SILENT NIGHT, UNHOLY BITES

AN IVY CREEK COZY MYSTERY

RUTH BAKER

CLEANTALES PUBLISHING

Copyright © CleanTales Publishing

First published in January 2022

All characters and events in this publication, other than those clearly in the public domain, are fictitious and any resemblance to real persons, living or dead, is purely coincidental.

Copyright © CleanTales Publishing

The moral right of the author has been asserted.

All rights reserved. This book or any portion thereof may not be reproduced or used in any manner whatsoever without the express written permission of the publisher except for the use of brief quotations in a book review.

For questions and comments about this book, please contact info@cleantales.com

ISBN: 9798401199607
Imprint: Independently Published

OTHER BOOKS IN THE IVY CREEK SERIES

Which Pie Goes with Murder?

Twinkle, Twinkle, Deadly Sprinkles

Eat Once, Die Twice

Silent Night, Unholy Bites

Waffles and Scuffles

AN IVY CREEK COZY MYSTERY

BOOK FOUR

1

"This is definitely my best time of the year," Lucy commented and glanced at her assistant, Hannah, who was sitting next to her, enjoying a cup of caramel flavored ice cream. "Does that taste good?"

"Hmm, this is so good. I can't tell you how stress-relieving this is," Hannah replied, taking another scoop of her ice cream.

Lucy had finished her cup of mint mixed with strawberry ice cream earlier, and watching Hannah indulge in hers made her crave more.

"You'll make me order some more," she said with a groan and stood up to retrieve some cupcakes from the kitchen for them to share. "You know, my mother used to make extra treats for the house during Christmas. On Christmas Eve, we spent it here at the bakery with my aunt, and anyone from the town who wanted to join us," she said, flashing Hannah a wistful smile. "I don't think that will happen this year."

Lucy gasped when Hannah finished the last scoop of her ice cream and punched her playfully on the arm. "Well, Christmas is all about making fresh memories, so I am sure this year we'll find something fun to do."

"Yeah," Lucy agreed and lowered her gaze for a bit. She raised her head when an idea slipped into her mind, and her lips widened into a grin. "I have an idea," she blurted out and jumped out of her chair.

Lucy paced around the open part of the dining area and propped her hands on her hips. "Decorating," she said.

"Decorating is your idea?" Hannah asked, scratching her head. "Doesn't everyone decorate at Christmas?"

"They do, but I meant decorating Sweet Delights. Putting up some lights and a Christmas tree. Then hosting a small party here for the local kids." Lucy could already imagine what it would look like on Christmas Eve, having kids over for some treats and then selling everything in the bakery at a discount. Maybe she could also take part in the seasonal bake fair.

Her mind was already buzzing with different ideas she could use to create a new tradition for Christmas this year. Her parents were no longer here, but she could never forget them, or the fun she had each year.

"Well, your plan sounds fun," Hannah agreed. "It will be nice to do some sort of bake sale too, you know. Ivy Creek's seasonal bake sale is a sure way to make money and then there's the publicity too because many families will reunite with their loved ones this season and you could get customers from out of town."

Lucy loved Hannah, and her brilliant ideas, but this time around she was really thinking about doing something purely fun. She shook her head, walked over to Hannah, and patted her shoulder.

"Do you even know how to have fun?" she teased.

"I'm more fun than you are, Lucy. Trust me," she replied, and they both burst into a fit of laughter. "Last year, I got my entire family presents for Christmas, and we went to the cinema to see a Christmas-themed movie before the carols on Christmas eve. What fun did you have on your end?"

Lucy remembered she still lived in the city back then, and she had done little. "I had a hot date," she replied, then stuck her tongue out at Hannah.

"What hot date? You're lying," Hannah replied, shaking her head as she turned away from Lucy.

The bakery door opened, and Hannah gathered the empty ice cream cups while Lucy welcomed the customer she recognized as the town's local pastor.

"Hello, Lucy," he greeted with a warm smile, his brown eyes settling on hers. "How are you?"

"I'm doing fine, Pastor Evans," she replied. "How are you doing? And your wife, Sarah?"

"Please, Noah is fine."

Noah Evans ran the town's local Baptist church Lucy and her parents attended when she was younger. The man had blessed her parents' marriage; he was also present when Lucy was born in the town's local clinic, and then again at her parent's funeral earlier that year.

In the years since she last saw him, he had aged. Most of his brown hair had streaks of white in it, and he had even gained a little weight.

"It's good to see you're doing well here, Lucy," he said.

"Is there something I can get you?" Lucy asked as she walked around the counter. Noah followed and placed both hands on the counter, leaning closer to it.

"Some cinnamon cake," he replied. "A church member dropped by my place and gave my wife and me some of your cinnamon cake and it tasted amazing. Reminded me so much of your mother's baking. She used to bring my wife and me pastries on Sundays when she had the chance, and I loved them."

The recipe also reminded Lucy of her parents. It was the first flavored cake she learned to bake when she turned sixteen, and she could never forget the look of pure joy on her parent's face when they tasted her baking for the first time.

"It reminds me of her, too," Lucy replied, and sealed up his paper bag. She handed it over to him, and he nodded as he took the bag from her. "I'm glad you enjoy them."

"Your mother would have been so proud to see how much you've accomplished here," he complimented, and looked around the bakery. "You're a tough one, Lucy Hale, just like your parents."

Lucy rubbed her palms together. "Thanks, Noah. I've added an extra chocolate cupcake for your wife. I remember how much she loves those."

"That's so sweet of you. You know the church made a tradition of giving out to the homeless and singing carols every Christmas. We'll be doing the same this year and it will be nice if you could bring us some treats and join in the entire event. It would feel nice to have you around, Lucy."

"What day is the event?"

"Sometime before Christmas," he replied, taking out some cash to pay for his order. "We stroll the streets singing carols and end up in the church or anywhere someone has volunteered to host us for the night. I think we would have the name of a host soon for this year's carol."

Lucy thought about contributing to the event for a second. She had just suggested creating a new Christmas tradition for Hannah, and this sounded like the perfect opportunity to do that. It would be more interesting because a lot of the citizens of Ivy Creek would take part in it and they could even meet new people—potential customers.

All she had to do was bake some treats and join in the fun.

"I'd love to bring some treats to the carol, Noah. If you inform me of a time and venue, I'll definitely work towards it."

"That's so nice of you, Lucy," he replied. "I'll sure let you know the venue. Happy holidays," he said and waved at her before making his way out of the bakery.

"Say hello to Sarah for me, and happy holidays," she called after him. Lucy's smile remained after he left the bakery.

Hannah returned to the dining area just then, and Lucy asked. "We're baking treats for the town's Christmas Carol night," she announced in a cheery tone.

Hannah dropped the pan of cookies she had already wrapped. "I heard Lucy. I just don't think it's such a great idea," she replied with less enthusiasm than Lucy expected.

"Why not? Sounds like fun and it's a good way to give back to the community. It will just be like Halloween when the kids go trick-or-treating. We will sing carols while walking from house to house, and afterwards, the participants would have a lot to feast on. Also, the homeless in town will enjoy some of our treats," she explained, already open to the idea. Lucy wanted Hannah to warm up to it too, as she joined her in arranging the packed cookies on the counter.

"I know it sounds like fun, but we could make sales here if we sell at the store instead of wasting our time on some road trip carol," she shrugged as she spoke. "I just don't think it's a good idea. Think about how many sales we might miss."

"Oh, come on! Loosen up a little. It's Christmas. We'd meet new people and advertise our products by sharing our treats. I am so positive about this, Hannah. It's something new to do over the holidays, a new tradition."

Hannah was quiet for a while before she released a defeated sigh that made Lucy reach out for a high five. "If you say so, then let's do it," Hannah said as she forced herself to smile.

"Trust me, it's Christmas, and we'll have fun doing this." She had known Pastor Evans for years, and this was the town's Christmas Carols.

What was the worst thing that could happen?

2

A few days later, Lucy woke up bright and early and had a spring in her step. She sang along to the lyrics of a pop song, and she moved her hips in rhythm to the song. She applied more frosting on the top of the cupcakes and perfected each one with care, while enjoying the tune playing in her head.

She took a step back when she finished with the frosting and clapped her hands together to admire her work. "Perfect," she muttered to herself, grinning as she admired the red and green Christmas-themed design on the cupcakes.

The kitchen door swung open, and she looked up to see Hannah walk into the kitchen carrying three shopping bags. Hannah paused when her gaze landed on the cupcakes arranged on the table in delivery paper boxes, and she lifted her eyes to Lucy's.

"Don't you think this is too much?" she asked, walking to meet Lucy where she stood at the table. "Oh, Lucy, how many cupcakes did you bake?"

"Maybe over a hundred," Lucy replied with a sheepish grin. She groaned when Hannah arched a brow.

"A hundred and fifty?" Hannah said as her eyes widened.

Lucy continued with a wave of her hand. "Come on, it's for charity, and besides, this is Christmas. You need to get in the holiday spirit and loosen up, Hannah."

"Oh, I'm loose," Hannah replied with a gentle shake of her head. "I went to a nearby clothing store today, and I got everyone at home a pair of pajamas."

"Pajamas? Really?" Lucy teased. "You got your parents, sister, and yourself... pajamas?"

"Yes," Hannah replied proudly as she strolled over to the counter. "In my family, we wear pajamas on Christmas morning, and sit in front of the decorated tree to open our presents—It's tradition."

"And you have to wear pajamas for that?" Lucy burst into laughter and shot Hannah an apologetic smile. "I don't mean to tease but, I think sharing cupcakes sounds better."

Hannah rolled her eyes and emptied the cup of water she held in the sink. "I'm happy to bake cupcakes for charity. I just think you might have gone overboard on this one."

Lucy sighed when Hannah came over to her and placed both hands on her shoulder. "Maybe you're too excited about this. Wait, let me guess... Richard Lester will be there, right? It's a town occasion, and his late relatives were huge donors to these kinds of events. Is that why you're so excited? Oh, my... are you trying to impress him?"

It was Hannah's turn to laugh, and Lucy punched her playfully in the arm before turning back to clean up the kitchen.

"Impressing Richard is the last thing on my mind. I'm doing this because Christmas is the time to share, and this is an opportunity to do that. Besides, we'd be giving out free treats. That means many happy bellies in Ivy Creek."

"Hmm, I believe you," Hannah replied, her eyes dancing.

Richard Lester popped up in her conversation with Hannah once in a while since Lucy went on her first date with him weeks ago. He ran a cafe in town, and Lucy enjoyed popping in there for some chamomile tea whenever she was in that part of town.

Lucy knew the tone of her voice suggested she didn't believe a word she just said, and she chuckled.

She finished cleaning the kitchen and hurried up to her apartment to get ready for the occasion. When she returned, Hannah had packaged the cupcakes and put them in the back seat of Lucy's car.

"Ready to go?" Lucy asked as Hannah locked the kitchen doors.

Hannah turned to her and replied in a sing-song voice. "You're wearing make-up, and you claim you're not trying to impress the man. Dream on, Lucy."

Hannah's statement ended with a laugh, and Lucy joined in as they headed out to her car so they could make it to the venue in time to watch the choir sing the Christmas carols.

Lucy sang along as the carolers belted out popular songs. She had set up a stand at the back of the tents set in the churchyard, and the attendance was more than Lucy expected.

She saw some people she hadn't seen in a while. Aunt Tricia, her mother's sister who recently moved back to town, sat close to her stand, humming along to 'Silent Night' as the pianist performed a solo. She also saw Becky Anderson, a businesswoman she worked with months back in the front row with some women, Lucy didn't know.

Lucy sucked in a deep breath. It was good she had attended the event. At least this way, she could blend in more than she already had. She angled her head towards the entrance again and saw Taylor, her ex-boyfriend, and the town's deputy sheriff walk in with his mother.

Lucy's heart warmed from watching the crowd. When she was younger, the town had celebrated like this during Christmas, but her parents hosted most of such gatherings, and it was usually a typical dinner hosted in the town's hall on the evening of Christmas Eve where they would sing songs, eat, and enjoy long discussions.

She believed things like this brought people together, and she was glad she had contributed to it.

"Having fun?" a voice asked behind her, and she turned to see Richard.

Lucy gave him a brief hug, and he pecked her on both cheeks, bringing heat to the back of her neck before he pulled away.

"Wow, you made a lot," he said, commenting on her full stand.

"What can I say? I love Christmas."

The carol ended minutes after Richard arrived, and people flocked towards her stand in pairs to get their fill of her treats. Lucy happily served them, alongside Richard and Hannah.

When most of them had received a cupcake, Pastor Noah Evans came to her stand with his wife, Sarah. Lucy greeted them both with a warm smile, hugging Sarah briefly.

"Thank you so much for doing this, Lucy," Sarah said. "You've made many people here happy."

"I'm glad I could be of help, and I'd do more anytime," Lucy replied.

Lucy's discussion with the pastor and his wife was interrupted when a lady walked up to them and asked Lucy in a curt tone. "Do you have any more treats other than what I see on this table?"

Lucy turned to the lady. "Hello," she said and handed her a cupcake.

The woman took it. "I mean, I need more," she continued briskly as she took a bite of the cupcake and chewed. "I run a shelter for homeless people, and a lot of them could not make it here today because, well, they couldn't afford to. Don't you think we should give them some treats, too?"

"Tabitha, take yours and let others have a taste of the treats," Sarah said before Lucy could reply.

"I wasn't talking to you," Tabitha replied. She hissed and looked at Lucy, her gaze flickering over her body. "I was talking to Miss Nice Pants over here."

Lucy blinked, taken aback by the woman's rudeness. Tabitha wore a sneer, and she didn't mind that people had stopped and were staring at Lucy's counter.

"I want more cupcakes for the hungry souls back at my shelter. This is charity, right? Then you don't mind showing the poor folks some kindness."

"Well, you can have some cupcakes for them," Lucy replied and masked her annoyance with a grin. She wanted nothing to spoil the cheery mood she was in.

Hannah was about to protest beside her, but she gave her a cautious look that made her stay put.

Lucy packed some cupcakes into a free box, added three extras, and handed it over to Tabitha. "Here you go."

"Is that it?" Tabitha asked as she snatched the box away. "Do you know what it means to be homeless? Surely you can't assume that this will be enough," she continued, eyeing Lucy.

Quietly, Lucy packed a dozen more cupcakes for her. She noticed a few people from the crowd had turned around to watch the scene, and she didn't want all the attention on her.

Tabitha collected the second pack. "You seem like a caring one, Miss Nice Pants," she remarked and her gaze dropped on the jeans Lucy wore. "Not everyone is as lucky as you folks," she hissed and pushed past Pastor Noah and his wife as she walked away.

"Well, that was some character," Lucy murmured when she was gone.

Noah and Sarah nodded in agreement. "I apologize on her behalf," Noah said.

"Oh, it's nothing. I just hope those cupcakes make some homeless person's day brighter," she replied and looked in the direction where Tabitha had departed moments ago.

Noah and Sarah said their goodbyes and moved on to talk to other people at the event while Lucy turned to Hannah and Richard. "This was fun, wasn't it?" she asked, her eyes mainly on Hannah because she wanted to see her expression.

"Oh, yes, it was," Hannah replied with a laugh. "I'm glad I came, but it doesn't trump my pajamas morning with the family."

They started packing up the stand. Aunt Tricia joined them as they rounded up, and she joined in their small talk about the event and how angelic the carolers sounded as they sang.

As they drove back to the bakery, a song about Christmas was playing on the radio, and they all sang along to the lyrics. Lucy was glad she found a new tradition for Christmas, and as she rounded the corner leading to the main street, she wondered about Tabitha and the homeless souls she had referred to.

Lucy wondered if the homeless would overlook Tabitha's brutish behavior and enjoy the cupcakes with gladness in their hearts.

3

The good vibes from the caroling event stayed with Lucy the rest of that evening. The next morning when she got down to the bakery, she met Hannah at the front counter taking notes from a man standing with his identical triplet daughters.

"You have really lovely little girls," Hannah complimented as she packaged his order of kale chips, bread, and a double latte espresso.

"Thank you, Hannah," he said and took the hand of the nearest girl. "My girls are a lot to handle on my own, but they're still a joy."

"I can see," Hannah replied with a chuckle, and Lucy joined her to wave as the man took his order and left the bakery.

Lucy walked over to Hannah and joined her in serving the other customers in line. Hannah took the orders while Lucy packaged them and handed them over before Hannah took the cash.

They worked like that in sync for a few minutes before the store emptied again. "We have a lot of customers trooping in today. I think word has spread about Sweet Delights and people are driving down from the far end of town to try out our pastries," Hannah said. "Turns out the charity work at the church paid off, even though we were giving away free cupcakes."

"I know, right," Lucy replied, and tucked her shirt into her jeans. "I'm glad it's working for us."

They went into the kitchen, and Hannah took out the notepad in the pocket of her apron. "We've got two deliveries this morning. One downtown, and the other at the police station. We don't have any available drivers to make the delivery. Do you think you could handle these two?"

"Of course," Lucy replied.

Hannah was saying something about deliveries, and she had lost track for a moment because her mind wandered, but she quickly re-directed her attention back to Hannah.

"Right, I will drive down to drop them off. When I come back, we can start working on the last order you just took from the man with the triplets."

"Mr. Johannesen?" Hannah said. "He's well known in town as the ever-dotting father. When his wife gave birth to the triplets, he stepped back from a 9-5 routine job, started a local business, and hired an operations manager to handle the day to day running of the business, while he spent time with his family."

"I admire him," Hannah said wistfully.

"You'll find your Mr. Right. Don't worry," Lucy told her.

She turned around to pick up the order Hannah had prepared on the table, and bent down to stroke her white Persian cat, Gigi, who had just sauntered in.

Lucy's heart melted when it purred, then flipped over to lie on its back. "I'll see you later, Gigi," she said and straightened again. She took the orders out with the note Hannah handed her and drove down to the station first to drop off the chips and cupcakes the officers ordered.

Lucy met a few of them standing outside the station when she arrived, and she handed over the package to Dan, an officer she knew.

"How are you, Lucy?" he asked as he paid for the order.

"I'm doing great, Dan. How are things around here? Is there a lot of trouble during the holidays?"

"Well, there's always trouble in Ivy Creek. We just try to do our best and hope no one spoils the fun for others."

"That's great work you do," she replied.

Lucy craned her neck and looked around a little, trying to see if she could spot Taylor. He hadn't come over to the stand yesterday to say hello, and she saw him leave after the carolers stopped singing.

Maybe he was in a hurry to get to work, she thought, and looked at Dan again. "I should go. I have deliveries to make."

"Bye, Lucy," he said, waving as she headed back to her car.

She drove to the second address, which was an office near the church building, and delivered the bread and macaroons. At the front desk, she noticed the receptionist opening a paper bag of cupcakes. He took one out after he handed her cash for the order, and the wrapper design caught Lucy's attention.

Lucy paused instead of walking away and edged closer to the table again.

"Hey," she said, gaining his attention. "You know, that cupcake looks delicious, and I'm wondering where I can get one for myself?"

"Oh, you can get one at a hotel right around the corner from here. I sometimes go there for breakfast and it was on the dessert menu today. The place is called Blue River, and it's not far off from here."

"That's very kind of you, thanks," Lucy replied before walking off.

Lucy drove down the road, rounded the corner, and saw the building with a big maroon sign in front. She went to the hotel and made her way inside.

The ground floor had a restaurant, dining room, and several conference rooms. She imagined the upper floors housed the rooms for guests. The hotel staff she walked past were dressed neatly in well-pressed shirts and matching pants, and she admired the city landscape paintings on the surrounding walls.

Lucy noticed they were running a buffet service when she saw the setting and display of dishes on a table by the far end of the dining room.

"Hello, what would you like? Our menu for the day is on the other side," the waiter said to her.

Lucy forced a smile. Her curiosity peaked when she saw more customers stroll towards the buffet stand and return with cupcakes.

Is this pure coincidence? Or is someone intentionally serving my cupcakes at this restaurant without my knowledge.

She headed for the buffet stand to see what else they had on the menu for herself, and she heard some customers whisper about how good the cupcakes tasted as they walked past her.

"I hope they serve them every day," one lady said to the other as they picked another cupcake from the display table.

"Hello, excuse me," Lucy called, tapping on the shoulder of the man in front of her in the buffet queue. "Do they serve these regularly?"

"No, it's the first time the owners brought them in," he replied. "They're really worth it. Try one… this is my third cupcake."

"I'd like to meet the owner. Do you know where I can find—"

The man pointed at the entrance before Lucy ended her question. She spun around to see the woman she met at the church the previous day, and her eyes narrowed to tiny silts.

"There she is. I guess she just came in."

"Thanks," Lucy murmured as the man walked away with his plate, and Lucy walked over to where she stood.

She took in her round frame, noticing she was quite bigger than she remembered from seeing her yesterday. She wore a red dress that did nothing to hide her rounded mid-section and full limbs. The look on her face was displeasing, and in Lucy's opinion, Tabitha would look a lot better if she tried to not frown or glare often.

"What you did was wrong. You know there were other people who could have benefited from my cupcakes, and what you did deprived them of it," Lucy said.

She jabbed a finger in Tabitha's direction and added with an unflinching stare, her anger bubbling higher. "I can't let you get away with this."

Tabitha flung her head back and cackled softly. "What will you do?" she asked, taking a step towards Lucy. "You can't do anything, Miss Nice Pants. You really thought I was going to give all those cupcakes to homeless people? You're gullible…. It's best you get out of my building, or I'll have you thrown out."

Lucy stood her ground, unwilling to let Tabitha have the final say. "This is deceitful," she accused again.

"Well, what are you going to do about it?" Tabitha tossed back, gently lifting one shoulder. "John, please see the young lady out of my building," she said, turning to the security man standing by the curve near the receptionist table.

The man led Lucy out of the building while she tried to walk as fast as she could. Outside, she bottled down a scream and got into her car.

As Lucy drove back to her bakery, she replayed the altercation she'd had with Tabitha and wondered why anyone would want to do something so mean.

4

As Lucy walked through the doors at Sweet Delights, she put a smile on her face to mask the rage she still felt bubbling on the inside. She noticed the bakery was full of customers and joined Hannah in attending to them.

They served the treats they had in stock, and at intervals, Hannah checked on the treats baking in the oven. Lucy's mind still spiraled with thoughts of how she could have handled her interaction with Tabitha. She knew some people would just say it was cupcakes, but it was more than cupcakes to her. She baked each cupcake, hoping it would bring some Christmas cheer to whoever ate them. It was never her intention for them to serve the purposes of a rude and lazy business owner.

"We'll need more supplies if we're going to bake these large amounts for the rest of the holiday," Hannah was saying as she took cash from a customer.

"That's right," Lucy said. She turned to the next lady in the queue. "What would you like to have?"

"A soy-caramel coffee please, and three gluten-free bread, and muffins."

Lucy smiled at her. "Coming right up."

"You know this place has delightful treats and I love coming here, but it's lacking one thing," the lady said as she accepted her order from Lucy.

Lucy leaned in towards the lady. "What's missing?" she asked, her eyes wide. *Did I forget an ingredient in my recipe? Or is there something missing from the dining setting?*

Lucy couldn't figure out what the lady was getting at until she saw a lopsided grin spread across her face.

"Christmas decorations!" she pointed out. "It's the holidays, Lucy. You can add a bit of color and decorations to spice the place up. It'll really make this place more inviting this time of the year," she added and tipped her plastic cup in Lucy's direction before walking away.

Lucy quickly looked around her bakery. The lady's suggestion made sense, and she made a mental note to put up some lights, trees, and fixtures to give the place a festive look for the season. She knew how decorations could alter the atmosphere around the bakery. Plus, putting them up would be fun.

When they finished serving the customers, Lucy let out a deep sigh and leaned over the counter.

"Are you all right?" Hannah asked her as she closed the cash register. "You look flushed, and you have this redness all over your ears. Did something annoy you?"

Lucy opened her mouth to recount the scene with Tabitha, but before she could say anything, Noah Evans stepped into the bakery wearing a full smile.

"Hello, Lucy. How is business today?"

"Great, Noah," she replied.

Hannah patted her shoulder and went into the kitchen while she focused her attention on Noah. "Would you like anything?"

"Yes, some macaroons please, and three coffee-flavored cupcakes. My wife won't stop craving them," he replied with a light chuckle.

"I'm pleased to know she loves them."

Lucy started working on his order, and he continued. "There's an award night event at the church tonight, and I dropped by to invite you. It's a celebration we do to appreciate members of the church and town folk who have contributed over the year."

Lucy handed him the paper bag containing his treats. "I don't know, Noah. Things are quite hectic here today, so I can't promise to attend."

"I understand," he replied, and handed her cash, taking his order. "I would love to have you around anyway, so if you can make it, please do."

"Okay."

"Have a nice day," he said and walked away.

Lucy watched the door swing shut behind him and she rubbed her eyes with both hands. Her cell phone buzzed in her pocket, and she picked it up on the second ring.

"Lucy, honey, will I see you for dinner at Christmas? I'm making plans, dear, and I'd like to have you and Hannah's family around," Aunt Tricia said.

"Christmas dinner sounds like fun, auntie," she replied.

"Great, dear. I'm attending the award night at New Baptist Church today. Are you coming?"

Lucy rubbed her temple. "I told Pastor Evans I'd consider it."

"All right, talk to you soon. Love you."

"Love ya," Lucy replied, and hung up.

Lucy heard Hannah calling her name, so she hurried into the kitchen to help her check on the items baking while Hannah frosted a birthday cake.

"Will you be attending the awards night at New Hope?" Hannah asked as she perfected the design, adding more color to give the cake more beauty.

"Um… not sure. Are you attending?"

"Yeah," Hannah responded. "My sister's presenting the awards alongside Sarah Evans, the pastor's wife."

"Interesting," Lucy said and went to the sink to wash her hands.

"You sure you're all right?" Hannah asked.

"Yeah, I'm fine," she replied, not wanting to bring up the drama she'd had with Tabitha. "I'll be right back," Lucy said and headed up the stairs to her apartment to use the restroom.

Later that evening, Lucy drove down to the church to attend the event. She had nothing better to do, and she figured she could pass time there. She went with some brownies and cupcakes to serve the guests and when she made her way into the auditorium, the first face she saw was Becky Anderson's.

"Lucy," the woman greeted and helped Lucy with the packs she held. "It's been a while. How have you been holding up?"

"I've been all right, Becky. How have you been? I haven't seen you around town in a while," Lucy replied as they reached a table in the back row and set her packs down on it.

She had done business with Becky Anderson months ago, and although it had ended on an unpleasant note with a guest getting murdered that same night after eating her cupcakes, Lucy still admired the woman.

"I left town for a while to clear my head, and just got back for the holidays."

"So, you're back permanently? Or will you be leaving again?" Lucy asked, dropping what she was doing to look into Becky's eyes.

"I'm back for good," she replied. "It feels good to have you around," Becky said as she patted the side of Lucy's arm.

"It's good to have you back, Becky. Hopefully, you'll stop by Sweet Delights to indulge in some festive treats. It will be on the house, so you can drop by anytime."

Becky's hand moved to her chest, and Lucy noticed the expensive jewelry she wore on her wrist and finger. "Thank you so much, Lucy. Enjoy the evening."

Becky walked away, and Lucy settled in a chair in the back row. She saw Hannah in front when she whipped her head around, and Lucy grinned, waving at her.

Hannah gave her a thumb's up and turned around to continue watching the event. Her sister was upfront on the pulpit giving a speech before she called out the first award for the night, and Lucy sucked in a deep breath, and smoothed a hand over the black, patterned dress she wore.

The speech dragged on for a while, and the crowd applauded before Sarah joined Hannah's sister Stacey in the pulpit.

"Now, it's time to give out the awards to those who've merited it for the year. We have a lot of wonderful families amongst us, and we appreciate everyone even though there isn't an award for everyone," Sarah said, and Lucy allowed her gaze to drift around the congregation.

A shiver raced up her spine. She couldn't understand it, but it made every part of her alert, like she was watching out for something, or expecting something to happen.

Whenever she experienced jittery nerves, something always went wrong in the end. Lucy swallowed and diverted her attention to the women on the stage.

"And the first award for tonight goes to the most dedicated member of the charity committee in Ivy Creek," Sarah said, then stepped back for Stacey to announce the winner.

"The award goes to Tabitha Alli."

The crowd gave a muted applause, and Lucy rolled her eyes as she watched Tabitha make her way to the front while enjoying a cupcake she held in one hand.

"Thank you, everyone," Tabitha said, waving. She took the wrapped award and waved again, but this time grinning. "This means a lo—" her words ended in a choke.

Tabitha coughed, and her hand moved to her neck before she slumped to the ground with a loud thud. Murmurs erupted amongst the crowd from different corners, and Sarah dropped to her knees to check on Tabitha on the floor.

"We need a doctor here," she called out with a frantic wave, her voice edgy.

Lucy remained rooted to her chair, unable to move as she watched the scene unfold. The fidgety movements and anxious whispers drowned every other thought, and adrenaline coursed through her.

Three men rushed to the pulpit. One of them said, "I'm a doctor, I'll check her."

Lucy watched the man drop to his knees, and seconds later when he raised his head, he announced in a chill voice that Lucy knew would stay in her head for a long time, "She's… she's dead."

5

The muffled murmurs turned to chaos after the announcement, but Lucy remained rooted to her chair, her heartbeat racing as people scurried to get out of the church auditorium. Mothers dragged their children towards the door, and others hurried out in pairs, not bothering to hide their fear as they screamed and pressed each other to get out.

Stacey still stood on the pulpit, her hands on her lips, and Lucy could see the terror in her eyes as she looked around. Pastor Evans and his wife were by Stacey's side, and the man who checked Tabitha seconds ago stood up from his crouching position.

"She has no pulse, she's dead," he said again.

Panicked voices and murmurs floated past her as the crowd dispersed, and her mind raced.

What just happened? She's dead? How did...

Lucy nearly screamed when a hand touched her. She bolted out of her chair, eyes wide, and lips slightly parted as she turned around to see Richard holding her arm.

"It's me," he said and came to stand beside her.

Lucy looked around the almost empty church, trying to find Hannah or her Aunt Tricia.

"We should get out of here," Richard suggested.

She shook her head. "No… I have to find Hannah and my aunt," she said, willing her head to stop spinning. When she saw Pastor Evans make his way towards where she stood, his eyes drawn together in a frown, she moved and met him halfway.

"I just called the cops," he began. "They're on their way here as I speak."

Lucy's hand moved to cover her mouth, and she asked in a shaky voice. "Is she really dead?" Lucy asked, still trying to wrap her head around what just happened.

Pastor Evans's eyes bored into hers, and she muttered, "Oh God."

Richard's hand came around her shoulder, and he pulled her closer to him. His fingers squeezed into her arm, and she shook her head again.

"Excuse me," Pastor Evans said and headed for the door.

Richard steered Lucy towards the exit. Her legs felt like jelly, and she couldn't stop the dreadful rumbling in the pit of her stomach.

They reached the door at the same time the police arrived. Three officers marched towards the church with quick steps and stopped them from exiting the building completely.

"No one else leaves till we get everyone's statement," one of them announced, spreading his arms to block Richard and Lucy's path.

"Miss, please step back into the building," the officer said to another woman trying to leave the church. The second cop went into the building, and Lucy turned back to Richard.

"Let's go back inside and give our statements," she said in a flat voice. She rubbed her sweaty palms on her sides as they walked towards the entrance. Lucy had a slow flight response; she could have raced out of the hall when Tabitha collapsed, but her body remained glued to the chair.

They walked over to the front, where Stacey and Sarah still kneeled beside Tabitha's lifeless body. The pale look on Stacey's face made the knots in Lucy's stomach tighten, and she took a deep breath to keep the rising nausea away.

Richard helped her to a seat, and he held her hand the entire time as they watched the cops talk to Stacey and Sarah at the pulpit. Lucy knew they would come to question her, and she braced herself for the questions.

She knew nothing about this. Just like every other person in the church, she witnessed Tabitha mount the front stage to speak and drop to the ground. The officers finished with Stacey and Sarah in a few minutes, and then they moved to two other women, then Pastor Evans, before they came to where she sat.

Lucy raised her chin a bit and licked her dry lips.

"Miss Hale?" the officer asked, and she responded with a slight nod. "Did you know Mrs. Alli personally?"

"No," Lucy replied. "We met for the first time at the town's Christmas carol."

"I understand you served the treats at the event tonight, and also at the Christmas Carol."

"Yes, I did." Lucy paused for a second. "What has that got to do with this?"

"We are simply covering all grounds, Miss Hale," the officer replied. He took out a notepad, and asked Lucy a few more questions about the treats she served, and if she had run into Tabitha before the start of the event.

"I met Tabitha recently."

"When was this? At the caroling event?"

"No. It was at her hotel."

"What did you think of her? Tabitha Alli, what was your relationship with her like?"

"We didn't have any sort of relationship," she replied quickly and felt Richard squeeze her hand slightly. Lucy tried to control her nerves. She knew where these questions were leading. These cops had a way of implying guilt. She had to be alert not to say anything incriminating.

She had been labeled a person of interest in a previous murder investigation in town simply because of her association with the victims before their death.

"Look, officer, I had nothing to do with this. Just like everyone else here, I'm in shock. I do not know what happened here, and I'd just—" she stopped to catch her breath. "I just want to leave this place."

"I understand that Miss, but we ask these questions as part of our job, and not to accuse you of anything," he replied, then rose to his feet. "We will be in touch if we need anything else."

"Thank you."

Hannah approached where she sat with Richard when the officers left, and she stood up again.

"God, this has been an eventful day," Hannah commented and wiped the hair on her forehead away. "How are you? What happened was shocking, yeah?"

"It was," Lucy agreed. She ran her fingers through her hair and bit her lower lip. "They don't know what happened yet?"

Hannah shook her head. They both glanced back towards the pulpit where Pastor Evans still stood with some officers, his wife, and three other men.

"Did they ask you anything about your treats?" Hannah asked.

"Yes, they did."

"I suspected they would. Someone mentioned they saw Tabitha eating some treats before they called her forward to receive the award. I just can't believe this happened here in church of all the places in town."

Lucy saw Hannah shudder. She had her own anxieties about the inevitable investigation that was already in motion over Tabitha's death and what that might entail. She had experienced it before, and she didn't want to again.

"This seems so surreal. I can't believe this is happening again," Lucy muttered. "Have you seen Aunt Tricia anywhere?"

"I think she left when everyone was rushing to get out."

"We should leave too," Richard chirped in.

Lucy realized her hand was still in his, and he squeezed it gently, looked at her, and gave her a tiny smile.

"Yes, we should."

They left the church. Lucy waved Hannah and Richard goodbye and got into her car to drive back home. On the route back to the bakery, she replayed the tragic scene that had occurred in the church in her head.

From what she could tell, Tabitha Alli was not exactly a model citizen of Ivy Creek, so it was possible she had lots of enemies, right?

Why would anyone want Tabitha dead? And who could it be? Or was her death due to natural causes?

Lucy tried not to think about it, but it was all that ran through her mind. She approached her bakery ten minutes later and parked her car in the back of the building. She got out and headed for her apartment upstairs.

Gigi greeted her when she reached her living room and followed her into the bedroom as she took off her clothes. "I'm so tired, Gigi," she murmured, picked up her cat, and settled in her bed.

With a deep sigh, Lucy made herself comfortable and stroked her cat's fur. Once again, someone had died in Ivy Creek, and somehow, she was linked to it.

Why does this always happen to me?

6

*L*ucy was absent-mindedly mixing a new batch of brownies when the front door opened, and Hannah walked into the kitchen seconds later. The previous night, she had tossed in bed for a while, thinking about Tabitha's sudden death before she finally fell asleep, and Lucy imagined what it would be like for her family right now.

She lost her parents earlier in the year, and it had been a rocky few months since then. Even if Tabitha wasn't an angel, her family still did not deserve to go through the heartache of losing her suddenly.

"Hey," Hannah greeted, and took off the satchel hanging on her shoulder. "Did you get any message of the award you won? The church sent out messages to the other recipients last night.

"You know we might receive an award too. Probably for serving the best treats in town, and making people happy," Hannah continued. She grinned at Lucy when Lucy stole a glance at her and continued. "Winning an award will help our business—expand it and help us gain more publicity."

"You think we would have won an award last night?" Lucy asked.

"Yes… I mean, we obviously deserve one."

Lucy continued sieving flour into a dry bowl for the brownies quietly as Hannah talked. "Well, I didn't get any message," she replied, then raised her head to meet Hannah's gaze. "Tabitha died yesterday, remember? And that ended the event. So, did they still give out awards after that?"

"They sent out messages this morning. My mother received one for the most active member."

"That's nice," Lucy said and reached for her phone in her apron to check. "Maybe I would get one, but so far, I haven't."

"Oh…" Hannah shrugged and joined her at the table and began gathering the items she needed to make cupcakes.

Lucy stopped sieving when Hannah started humming and faced her. "I just can't get Tabitha's face out of my head. What happened was tragic."

"Truly," Hannah replied. "My sister kept talking about it this morning and I couldn't hang around to hear her say more. She said the cops have started their investigation."

Hannah's statement about the investigation made Lucy's throat tighten, and she continued her sieving again. Minutes later, brownies were in the oven, and she had moved on to another task.

They worked together in silence for a while till she heard someone call for her in the front and went out to attend to the customers.

"Good morning. What would you like to get?"

"Three macaroons, please," the young customer replied, her gaze fixed on the display glass. "Make that four, I can't seem to get enough of your pastries."

Lucy attended to a few more customers, and she sold the rest of the cupcakes available, and some bread before she returned to the kitchen to join Hannah again.

"We have a delivery to an office downtown," Lucy said as she bent over the oven to check the brownies. Her recipe always required minimal heat and a little longer baking time because she always tried to avoid burned pans, so she checked to make sure the heat was reduced, and she set the timer.

"They ordered brownies, cupcakes, and coconut bread this morning, and they need their order by evening today."

"Where is the place?"

"Same place I delivered bread to at sixth avenue three days ago. Their office complex is just by Blue River Hotel."

"Right, Blue River Hotel," Hannah replied. "Tabitha owns that place. I wonder if it's open today, you know, after yesterday's tragedy."

"Maybe we can run this delivery together if we finish selling early today, so we drop by Aunt Tricia's place?" Lucy didn't want to drive around that zone alone. If the cops had started their investigation, then they would be around the hotel today.

"That sounds like a great idea. I also want to know what she thinks about what happened last night. It's all the town can talk about."

Lucy shook her head and continued working in the kitchen. Unlike Hannah, she didn't want to think about Tabitha's case at all. She remembered the last personal contact she had with Tabitha, and that she had been offended with her for what she did with the cupcakes she took from her at the Christmas carol. Who else had Tabitha offended? Was the offense so egregious that they wanted her dead?

She pushed Tabitha out of her mind. "Let's just try to finish up work early today," she suggested.

By midday, they closed the bakery to head out to the address where Lucy was to deliver three coconut loaves with three dozen cupcakes with sprinkles.

"That's Tabitha's hotel," Hannah commented as Lucy drove past Blue River Hotel, as she approached her destination and parked her car.

"I will be right back," Hannah said as she got out, and picked the delivery basket from the back seat. Lucy watched her disappear into the building, and she closed her eyes for a second, tapping her fingers on the steering wheel.

When she re-opened her eyes, she glanced toward Blue River Hotel. The hotel was open, and people were walking in and out of the building.

Lucy wanted to remain inside the car, but she couldn't, not after she noticed the hotel was open for business even after what happened to its owner the previous day.

She got out of her car and walked to the front of the building. Standing by an enormous tree in front of the building, she crossed her arms over her chest and pinned her gaze on the sliding doors in front of the building.

Two women stepped out of the hotel holding paper bags, and Lucy shifted her weight from one foot to the other. She knew it was not her business, but she didn't expect that the hotel would be open when the owner just passed away.

She wondered how the staff inside would feel about Tabitha's death. Most of them would have worked with her for some time, and she imagined they would be in a state of shock.

How was Tabitha to her workers? Was she also rude and overbearing to them?

Lucy imagined what it would be like to work for a woman like Tabitha. She was certain she wouldn't be able to stand her personality or even endure working for her.

She didn't know how long she stood there and wasn't aware that someone had been standing beside her until she heard a voice.

"I can't believe she's gone."

Lucy turned to see a man standing next to her. He was tall and dressed in a black winter jacket with a tartan scarf wrapped around his neck. He offered her a half-baked smile that didn't reach his brown eyes, and Lucy saw his throat bob when he spoke.

"Life is so short. One day you're making plans for the future and the next you're no more. I'm still trying to come to terms with the fact that Tabitha is no more."

"I didn't know her well, but it's sad what happened," Lucy said and turned to the building again.

On both occasions she had met Tabitha, the woman had been rude and inconsiderate, and she wondered if that was how she regularly carried herself. If she was always that way—arrogant and loud, then how did she get along with anyone?

Without thinking, Lucy voiced her inner thoughts about Tabitha. "I wonder what happened, but then again, considering she was rude and greedy, it's no surprise that someone wanted her dead and killed her, right?"

Lucy didn't look at the man by her side as she continued. "A woman as rude as her would have made a lot of enemies, even in a small town like Ivy Creek, don't you think? I met her twice, and she was not pleasant in the interactions I had with her."

She saw the man shake his head from the corner of her eyes and finally glanced at her side to stare at him. His eyes bulged out, and he clenched his jaw hard as he stared at her. She saw his nostrils flare.

"I'm sorry… I don't think we've met before. I'm Lucy Hale," she said and extended a hand to him.

He accepted her gesture, but the hard-line on his lips didn't ease a bit, and his grip on her hand was tight as he said in a gruff voice. "Nice to meet you, too. I'm Justin Alli."

"Alli?" Her jaw went slack, and she croaked as she forced her hand out of his. Her cheeks instantly burned as heat rose there from the back of her neck. She remembered the words she just said about Tabitha and groaned inwardly.

Her stomach rolled over when he swayed his head gently and spoke. "Yes, I'm Tabitha's husband."

7

"Oh God, I'm so sorry," Lucy said as she took a step back. She made a slight hand gesture as she continued, not giving Justin the chance to say anything. "I didn't mean to speak ill of the dead, and I meant nothing I said in a bad way."

Justin's frown eased a little. "It's all right. I'm Tabitha's husband, and I know my wife was a handful," he said in a solemn voice. Justin slipped both hands into his pockets, and Lucy bit her lower lip. "She was difficult to work with, and not so friendly with people. What you said is nothing I haven't heard before."

His flat tone and cracked voice made Lucy's heart stutter. She lowered her head, feeling remorseful. "I'm really sorry," she said again.

Justin lifted his shoulder in a slight shrug.

"I shouldn't have said what I said."

"It's okay, Lucy," he said. "If you don't mind, you can come in with me, and I'll show you around the hotel. I know we've only just met, but somehow I feel like I have to show you the woman Tabitha was beneath the rude exterior she showed others."

Lucy nodded. "Sure, I'd like to see Blue River."

Justin led the way, and Lucy slipped her keys into the pocket of her wool jacket before following Justin into the building. He showed her around the ground floor where they had the reception and took her to a large waiting lounge.

Lucy admired the expensive chandelier in the middle of the foyer that brought the place alive, and she noticed the well-dressed servers carrying trays with glasses on them around the place.

"This is where most of our guests have dinner if they don't want room service," Justin said as she looked around the place.

At the corner of the room, someone sat in front of a huge piano and played a classical tune that the customers seemed to enjoy.

"This place is lovely," she complimented and he pointed to the stairs leading to the rooms. "I never imagined that it would be this big."

"We also have a bar and there's a games room for young families. Would you like me to show you the bar?"

"Yes, please," she replied.

He showed her the bar, and Lucy admired the dimly lit room. The bar was half-empty as most of the customers were still interested in the buffet and silver style service the restaurant offered.

"We got the property from a couple who wanted to move out-of-town years back, and Tabitha's hard work helped build it into what it is today. It might not be as big as what one would find in the city, but it was her life's work.

"We have some smaller rooms we offer at subsidized prices for those who can't afford our standard rooms. It's more like a place for them to rest at night, without having to worry about the high fees."

"I didn't know that," Lucy said.

They left the bar and headed back to the reception area. The elevator door opened as they walked past it, and a couple walked out hand-in-hand, waved at Justin, and walked into the restaurant to take a seat.

"I know you didn't," Justin replied.

Lucy felt another pang of guilt for what she said about Tabitha outside. Her first impression of the woman had led her to say that, but her husband seemed gentle and more jovial with the guests and staff.

She noticed he waved at some servers as they walked around, and a female worker who walked past them smiled at him. "Hello," he whispered to the lady before giving Lucy his attention again.

"Thanks for showing me around. I've only been here once, and I didn't make it past the outer reception where you have the buffet."

"You're welcome, Lucy."

He took her back to the buffet section, and she was about to thank him for the tour when a woman called for him.

"Yes?" Justin responded, and they both turned to see the woman approach them.

"There's someone on the phone for you, sir," she said when she reached where they stood, and Justin gave her a soft nod.

He turned to Lucy and spoke. "Please excuse me for a few minutes. I have to take this call. I'll be right back."

"No problem," Lucy replied, and he hurried away with the woman.

She looked around and headed towards the buffet display stand. There was a queue of three people by it, and she wandered close to it. Lucy saw someone dressed as a chef step out from a door to her left, and when the lady went back in, she followed.

Inside the kitchen, the scent of different spices hit her nostrils all at once. She saw the cooks hurry around trying to get everything ready for lunch, and Lucy admired the spacious and simple setting of the kitchen.

She saw one cook bring out a whole chicken from the oven, and another slid in a huge tray of chicken thighs. Chopping sounds filled the room, and the atmosphere was hotter than the rest of the hotel. Lucy had wiped a bead of sweat that was forming on her forehead.

It seems like they make a lot of sales here every day. They're cooking quite a large amount of food.

She stood by the doorway watching the scene till she felt a light tap on her shoulder. "Justin?" she called as she spun around.

Lucy gasped when she saw a woman's frown instead of Justin. She stared back into the stern dark eyes of the woman, and her breath hitched in her throat when the woman's hand formed a grip around her hand.

"What are you doing in here?" the woman asked.

8

Lucy yelped as the woman led her out of the kitchen to the outer corridor. She watched her shut the door behind her, then glare at her again. She took in her fierce dark eyes and the square jut of her chin.

"Who are you, and why are you lurking around here?" she asked.

Lucy searched her mind for words as the woman released her. "I was just… I'm sorry, I didn't mean any harm. I just wandered around and wanted to see what the kitchen was like," Lucy began explaining as the woman's jaw tightened further. She saw the lines on her forehead crease, and she folded her arms over her chest.

"The kitchen area is restricted and as a guest you shouldn't wander that far or else security will show you out."

"I'm really sorry," Lucy said again, wondering how many times she would apologize today. First off, she had almost offended Justin with her comment about Tabitha, and now this lady was glaring at her like she had committed a crime.

Her cheeks burned, and she extended a hand, hoping an introduction would lighten the mood. "I didn't mean any harm," she said to the female staff staring at her with wide, furious eyes. "I just got carried away because the kitchen smelled so nice. I'm Lucy... Lucy Hale. I run a bakery in town. It's called Sweet Delights."

At the mention of Sweet Delights, she saw the frown on the woman's face slowly disappear.

"You're that Lucy Hale?" she asked in an almost breathless voice before accepting Lucy's handshake. "Oh... I'm a huge fan of your bakery, an obsessed fan of your treats. It's nice to meet you. I'm Zara. Zara Stanmore," she continued and raised a hand to her chest. "Forgive me. I didn't know you were the owner of Sweet Delights. I hope I didn't appear rude to you."

"Of course not," Lucy replied, relief flooding through her. She laughed and shook her head. "It's nice to meet you, Zara."

"I'm the chief cook here, and I get worked up when things don't go according to plan," she continued, and Lucy noticed her shoulders slumped a little. "I keep everyone on their toes, so they don't mess up the meal schedule for the day."

"Must be a lot of work," Lucy responded. "It gets quite hectic when I work in the bakery too, and I barely keep it together with the help of just one employee. You seem to handle things here pretty well."

"I try my best, but yes, it does get a tad hectic. I've always wanted to meet you in person. I sometimes order treats from your bakery and also get them whenever I drop in at the grocery store. They always taste amazing, better than anything I've ever had."

"Thank you, Zara," Lucy said, blushing at the compliment. "I work hard to make sure my customers stay happy. It's the only way I can grow the business."

"Oh, tell me about it," Zara commented wryly, twisting her lips to a corner as she spoke. "I've always tried to make a strong point of making sure customers are happy, but it never seems to fly around here."

"What?"

She waved a hand at Lucy. "I mean, you obviously have a good work ethic, and appreciate your customers by making sure you give them the best. This hotel would be the premier hotel in town if we worked that way."

Lucy adjusted the sleeve of her jacket and rubbed the back of her neck. Zara's last statement intrigued her, and she wanted to know what exactly she meant.

Did Blue River have a history of not satisfying its customers?

"What do you mean?"

"Let's just say the customer isn't always right around here," Zara offered and shook her head. "Don't mind me. I should get back to work. I'm glad we met, Lucy," she said, then turned and pushed her way into the kitchen.

The door closed again, and Lucy spun around to see Justin approaching.

"Hey," she said, noticing he was staring right at the door.

"Were you just with Zara?" he asked.

"Yes, I ran into her, and we talked for a while," Lucy replied. "She's a gracious lady."

Justin directed her to the main exit, and when they got outside, she turned to him. "Thanks for the tour, Justin. You have a really nice place here."

"You're welcome, Lucy, and please, drop in anytime. I'll be more than happy to entertain you."

Lucy smiled at him as she turned to make her way towards her car. As she got closer, she noticed Hannah had returned, and she was sitting on the bumper of the car.

"There you are," Hannah said when Lucy got to the car. "I was wondering where you ran off to."

"I went to check out Blue River," Lucy replied. "It's surprising to see the hotel open for business after what happened yesterday."

"Shocking right?" Hannah said and got off the bumper.

Lucy opened the driver's side of the car, and as she got in, she glanced back at the hotel building to see Justin standing out front with Zara. She kicked the engine to a start and put the car in drive.

Before she drove off, she noticed that Justin and Zara were deep in a conversation, and it seemed quite heated when she saw Justin jab a finger at Zara and then at the hotel building.

I wonder what that was about; she thought as she made a turn and drove past the front of the hotel.

As the car bounced down the road, Lucy saw Justin and Zara through the rear-view mirror, still arguing.

9

When they returned to the bakery an hour later, Hannah went into the kitchen to bring out the already baked cupcakes. Lucy helped her display them, and they fell into another rhythmic round of work as customers began trooping into the bakery again.

"What took you so long when you went into Blue River Hotel?" Hannah asked as Lucy arranged a paper bag full of brownies and cupcakes for the customer in line.

"I met Justin Alli, Tabitha's husband. He was a gentleman."

Hannah frowned, and Lucy added. "He showed me around their hotel and offered to host me anytime I dropped by."

"Wow," Hannah replied, but Lucy sensed some cynicism in her tone before she continued. "That's interesting. You know what they say about birds of the same feather flocking together... I assumed he'd be as mean as his wife."

Lucy lifted a shoulder. "Well, he's real nice."

She continued serving the customers in silence, and Hannah did the same. When they finished serving the customers in the queue, Lucy leaned against the standing counter behind her. "The hotel is really beautiful and bigger than I imagined."

"Have you been there before?" Hannah asked.

Lucy nodded. "Yes, once when I made a delivery to that building before the award night at the church. I didn't make it past the reception because Tabitha was rude to me."

Hannah rolled her eyes. "As expected, she has the reputation for being that way."

Lucy sighed and remembered the warmth in Justin's eyes as he took her around the building, and the way he spoke to the guests who greeted him. He seemed genuinely nice, so it made her wonder what caused his argument with Zara.

Could it be about me?

Lucy pushed down the thought the minute it entered her mind. "I also met the head chef there, and you saw their argument, right? It didn't seem like they get along much."

Hannah turned away from her. She began clearing out the plates in the dining area because the bakery had emptied again. "I don't think we should concern ourselves with what goes on there. After the treatment you got from her and the hassle a potential murder investigation into her death might cause, I think we should just keep to ourselves."

"Still, she was someone's wife, maybe mother and relative. I could tell Justin was struggling just from looking at him. It must be so hard on him, and the staff who would still be in shock from what happened yesterday," she said, standing up straight to ease the tension in her back. "I think it's remarkable that Justin is trying to keep it together and run the business," she added.

"Well, your problem is that you care too much," Hannah pointed out before entering the kitchen.

Lucy followed her. "Come on, Hannah, show a little sympathy," she urged. "Think about what it would feel like to lose a loved one, regardless of how horrible the person's personality was. You would still care for them, wouldn't you? It's the same for Tabitha and her family. They'll miss her even though she wasn't the nicest person in the world."

Lucy grabbed a cup to pour herself water, and she wiped her lips with her sleeves when she finished drinking. "You should still show a little compassion."

"You're right," Hannah finally agreed. She pulled out a chair, lowered herself into it, and folded her hands under her chin. "It must be so sad for them."

"Yes."

"But still… I wouldn't feel compassion for Tabitha directly. Her family, I can feel sorry for, but not Tabitha. I know it sounds harsh, but come on, you can't honestly tell me it's shocking someone would want her dead? She must have offended the wrong person, and it led to this."

"That is also true."

"Hello…" someone called from out front, interrupting their discussion.

Both Lucy and Hannah hurried out of the kitchen to attend to the customer.

"What can I get you?" Lucy asked after exchanging pleasantries with the lady.

"Have you got any muffins?"

"Yes, we do."

"Three muffins to go please, and I'd like a slice of coffee cake with that."

"Okay."

Lucy packaged the order and handed it over to her before collecting a cash payment.

"You know, it's time you brighten up this place with some music," the lady commented as she took the receipt Lucy handed her. "It's a festive season. Surely you've got some decorations and music to bring this place to life and give it that holiday vibe?"

"Yes, I do," Lucy replied, and offered her a smile. "In fact, I plan to put some of those up today, so don't worry."

"You do that." The lady grinned at her and bent her head to inhale the pastries in her paper bag before leaving the bakery. Hannah joined Lucy where she stood and crossed her hands over her chest.

"I guess we should go shopping for some Christmas decorations, right?"

"Yeah," Lucy replied. She picked a napkin and began wiping the counter clean as they had finished their sales for the day, while Hannah went to the side of the dining area where they had a speaker, and stepped on a chair to reach it.

"I think it's broken," she said after a few seconds and stepped down from the chair. "We will need a new one because I can't get this one to play."

"I'll get one from the electronic store, but I don't think the store will be open this late," Lucy replied and glanced at the watch on her left wrist. "I'll just have to pick them up tomorrow."

"I think they stay open till much later now because of the holidays. My sister came in late last night with some items she got from there, so we could check to see if it's still open."

"Sounds like a plan. I'll drive by there tonight," Lucy said.

They cleaned up the bakery and made notes of what they would bake the next day before they closed the store for the night. Minutes after Hannah left for the day, Lucy picked up her purse and keys and headed out of the bakery.

She hummed a Christmas carol to herself as she got in the car and drove off. *It is time to put the bakery in a festive mood.*

10

Lucy walked along the aisles in the electronic store and tried to find the right speaker she could get for the bakery. She checked the price pasted on each unit and admired the shiny outlook of most of them.

Most of the speakers were quite fancy and expensive, but she didn't just need fancy or expensive. She needed something durable for the bakery, as it wasn't for her personal use.

What do I choose?

As she surveyed what was on offer, she scratched her head as she tried to figure what to choose. Lucy turned when she heard footsteps behind her, and a salesman grinned at her when he got close enough for her to hear him.

"Hello, can I assist you with anything?" he asked.

Lucy saw his name tag on the pocket of his shirt.

"Yes, I just can't make a choice," she replied, and shifted her gaze from his face to the speakers in front of her. "What do you suggest?"

"Most of the brands on this line are made of IP67 waterproof features, with 15 hours playtime, and integrated with Bluetooth. It has quality dust and waterproof features. It'll set you back about two thousand dollars," he said casually as Lucy tried to hide her shock at the price he had quoted.

"On this other end, we have premium quality speakers at a higher price, but they've all been slashed by about a thousand dollars. These speakers here can serve the purpose of longer play time, and higher bass intensity when you want to get the party started. I can test them out to show you how good they are if you like."

Lucy cleared her throat and offered him a waning smile. "Actually, you don't need to test it out for me. I'm looking for something less expensive and durable too. It's for my store, and I don't think I need something excessively loud."

One of the man's brows shot up, and he continued talking, completely ignoring her last statement about what she wanted. "We have something a little under a thousand dollars if you prefer to spend less. You can be the proud owner of Zealot speakers which are currently nine hundred and ninety-nine dollars and have a one-year warranty on them," he said and she followed him towards the line of speakers he was referring to.

"These are the best prices and products I can offer you, and you have to make a choice on one of these soon."

Lucy pressed her finger to the side of her lip. "Great, thanks for your help. I'll make a choice, and let you know," she replied and turned away from him to check out other products.

He followed, walking behind her as she began searching for a speaker a lot cheaper. His suggestions were perfect if she needed a speaker for a nightclub, and not for a store where people wanted to have intimate conversations with their friends and loved ones while they ate one of her treats.

"I think you should let me show you how great the Zealot speakers are." The man resumed talking behind her, and Lucy had to mentally restrain herself from snapping at him.

"That's unnecessary. Thanks for offering to help me make a choice, but I've got this."

"Miss—"

"Can you please leave, and I'll let you know once I make a choice?" she cut in before he said anything else.

Does he have to badger me to make a choice?

She exhaled when he stormed away from her and continued her search. A few seconds passed, and Lucy turned around when she felt a gentle tap on her shoulder.

"Hi," a gentleman staring down at her said when she raised her head to meet his gaze. "Sorry to bother you, but I kind of overheard your conversation with the salesman and I thought I should make a suggestion."

Lucy rubbed the back of her neck as she tried to avoid eye contact with him.

"Please come with me," he said when Lucy said nothing, and she followed him to the last aisle. "These are the best speakers you can use for your store. I've tried them personally, and they are durable, and not so expensive."

Lucy looked down at the price tag. "Five hundred," she murmured and looked at him again. "Thanks a lot for this suggestion."

"You're welcome, Lucy," he said.

Her eyes widened when he mentioned her name, and her jaw dropped. "How... how do you know my name?"

He gave her a face-splitting grin. "I saw you earlier today when you came into Blue River Hotel with Justin, and I heard your name when you introduced yourself to Zara, the head chef. I'm Reggie Wade."

"Hello, Reggie," Lucy said and matched his smile. "You work at Blue River?"

"Yes, I've worked there for a long time."

"It was a tragedy what happened, and I hope you're not too shocked yourself or devastated."

"It came as a shock to everyone, but we are taking it in stride and holding it together. Your visit caused a stir today after you left."

"What do you mean?" Lucy asked. She fixed her gaze on him, wondering if the stir had to do with the argument between Justin and Zara, which she had witnessed as she drove away.

"What kind of stir? Why, what happened after I left?"

Her questions lay unanswered. She sensed his hesitation when he licked his lips and slipped his hands into his pockets. "I don't think I should say anything."

"Why? You can't leave me hanging," Lucy probed, and she noticed the way his eyes darted around. He took a step away from her like he wanted to retreat, and she reached forward to stop him with her hand.

Slowly, he rubbed his chin, and she repeated the question. "Did it have something to do with me?"

11

Reggie stared at her intently, but the frown forming on the corner of his lips made Lucy realize his reluctance to answer her questions. She wasn't going to let that stop her. "Tell me, Reggie. Was it something I did?"

"No, no," he replied with a wave of his hand. "Look, I don't want you thinking it has anything to do with you because it doesn't, but…" he paused, and released a quick sigh. "Most of the staff didn't like Tabitha much."

"Wow! Shocker," Lucy breathed out under her breath. "That's expected. I didn't like Tabitha very much on our first meeting, either. She was plain rude and unwelcoming."

"Yeah, well, she was like that with everyone," he replied. "She bullied the staff at every chance she got. She always undermined our work, and never let us do anything without injecting her ideas, even when it wasn't her area of expertise." He paused and looked left and right before he continued. "She did it to her husband as well, always disrespecting him in front of everyone. It was quite emasculating. I have to mention that some of us are quite relieved she won't be around anymore, even though I know it's a horrible thought."

"Was she this way with customers too?" she asked, wanting to know more about Tabitha. The Blue River staff did not like her from what she learned from Reggie, and even though her husband did not speak ill of her when they met, was it possible that he also harbored some ill feelings towards his wife?

"She was," Reggie replied. "Blue River is a pleasant hotel, with better infrastructure than most of the hotels in town have. That is why most of the staff still work there. Its reputation keeps it going. Besides that, no one would want to work there."

"Zara, the chief cook, had a lot of conflict with Tabitha, mostly. As far as Tabitha was concerned, she always did something wrong."

"It must have been hard working there," she sympathized.

"You don't know the half of it."

Lucy probed again when it seemed like Reggie had relaxed around her a bit. "So why did my visit cause a conflict? I met Zara Stanmore, and she seemed like a wonderful woman. I hope I didn't cause any ruckus or argument?"

She remembered seeing Zara and Justin having a heated conversation as she drove away, and her interest piqued higher.

"I really shouldn't say." Reggie shifted his weight from one foot to the other. His lips parted slowly like he was about to say something else, but his phone rang in his pocket, and he reached for it. "I should go, Lucy. It was nice speaking with you," he said and turned away from her.

She watched him walk away, wondering why he was so cagey with what happened at the hotel. She turned back to the line-up of speakers to make a final choice on what she wanted to purchase.

With no further thoughts, Lucy picked the brand Reggie suggested and noted down the name. She walked around the aisle and headed to the cashier's stand to place her order.

Why was Reggie being so shifty?

As she got to the front, she saw him step outside the swinging doors. A few customers had walked into the store again, and a slow Christmas carol was booming in the background, elevating the mood inside the shop.

Lucy stopped at the counter and leaned forward to speak with the female cashier. "Hi," she said with a wide smile. "So, I came in to get a speaker and I finally made a choice. I would like to pay for it."

"Great! What brand is that? I'll check the price and print out a receipt for you."

"The brand name is Bose, and I believe it's the 251 range."

The cashier keyed in the name while she waited, and when she looked up at Lucy again, she wore a grin. "Right, we've got it for five hundred dollars. Would you like to make payment now?"

"Yes, please."

She reached into her wallet for her card and handed it over to the cashier. Lucy saw the sales representative she spoke with earlier step out of an inner office with another man, and when he spotted her, he hurried towards the counter.

"Have you made a choice, Miss?"

"Yes, I'll go with the Bose 251," she responded without taking her gaze off the cashier processing her payment.

"I suggested three other better brands for you. A little higher in price, but of better durability than what you went for. I think you should go for those," he began.

"I prefer the choice I made," Lucy quickly said before he went on about why she should listen to him.

"But Miss—"

"The young lady is entitled to her choice," the man who stood with him seconds ago cut in as he came towards the counter. He offered Lucy an apologetic smile after shooting a stern gaze at the rep. "Please forgive his approach. I'll come by tomorrow morning to install the speaker of your choice. Just leave your address with the cashier."

"Thanks," Lucy said. She retrieved her card from the cashier and scribbled down her bakery's address on the book provided.

"Have a beautiful night," the cashier said and Lucy waved at her one last time as she headed out of the store.

When Lucy stepped out of the store, she spotted Reggie standing in a corner to the left. He leaned on the wall behind him, with his head lowered, so he didn't notice when she came out.

"I'm sorry it had to end that way, but maybe it's for the best," she heard him say. "Think about it… now we don't have to worry about any of that again."

Lucy thought about going to him for a second, but she shook the idea out of her head and headed to her car parked by the curb. It was already late, and she had to make it back home in time to rest and prepare for work the next day.

As she got in her car and headed back home, she thought of her conversation with Reggie the entire time, and what she overheard him saying as she came out of the store.

What was for the best? What if Tabitha's death wasn't an accident, as everyone thought? And if it turned out it was intentional, did Reggie have something to do with it?

Something didn't sit right about the entire situation with Lucy, but she didn't want to make any wild guesses. She had done enough guessing when it involved cases like this in Ivy Creek in the past, and it always ended up with her getting entangled in something she knew nothing about.

This time, she planned to stay out of it and let the cops do their job. Whatever happened to Tabitha, it was their duty to find it out.

12

"Aunt Tricia, I think these should go on the tree," Lucy said, peering into a box of old decorations she found in her apartment upstairs. She remembered her parents had gotten them many years ago and used them every Christmas season. She used to love looking at the tree with elves and socks hanging around. It made the tree come alive, and she was glad she found them.

"They should," Aunt Tricia agreed and took the box from her. She placed it on a table and together they started bringing out the old decorations.

It wasn't fully dawn yet, and Aunt Tricia had stayed over the previous night to help her with the decorations that morning. Lucy also had a lot of baking to do as she had deliveries for the grocery stores and also some out-of-stock pastries she had to replace.

She was humming *12 Days of Christmas* to herself as she wiped the plastic elves clean, and Aunt Tricia joined her to hang them on the tree she just got. When they finished, the only thing they hadn't done was to hang the lights.

Lucy went into the kitchen to check the batter she was mixing with her electric mixer for cupcakes and reduced the speed to give it time to mix properly. When she came out front again, Aunt Tricia was standing on a chair. She was trying to hang the lights on the ceiling board, but even with the chair as an aide, she still couldn't reach the ceiling board.

"I think we will need help for that," Lucy said as she held onto the chair to keep it stable. She stopped humming when Aunt Tricia got down from the chair and put her hands on her hips.

"We've transformed the place, but the lights will make the place look magical, and that is just what we need right now," she said and looked around the bakery.

Lucy had put some lights on the display counter where she kept pastries for sale, and outside the bakery, she had put out some lights on the front door. All that was left were the speakers which she had purchased earlier and putting up the lights, which neither of them could handle.

Still contemplating on how they could do the last bit of their decorations, both ladies spun around when they heard the soft creak of the front door as it swung open.

"Taylor," Aunt Tricia chimed when they saw Taylor, the town's deputy sheriff, walk in. Her aunt went to him before he got to the center of the dining area, and she enveloped him in a hug. "How are you? It's been a while," she continued with an easy laugh.

Taylor wore a smile that reached his eyes as he looked from Aunt Tricia to Lucy. "I have to say, I love what you've done with the place," he complimented, and his smile widened.

Lucy acknowledged him with a soft nod of her head when he released Aunt Tricia and walked over to where she stood.

"How are you, Lucy?" he asked.

"Great! Just trying to get in the festive spirit, you know," she remarked.

His gaze dropped to the lights she held, and he tipped his head to one side. "Need help with that?" he asked.

"Yes, please." Lucy handed him the lights, and he strode to the chair, and placed one foot on it.

"Thank goodness you dropped by. We were just thinking of how to get that up ourselves," Aunt Tricia said and came to stand beside Lucy.

They both crossed their arms over their chests and watched Taylor drape the festive lights over the board with the adhesive cable hooks.

"I was driving back from the station, and noticed the lights inside were on, so I thought to drop by and say hello," Taylor replied, and cast a glance at Lucy over his shoulder before he focused on his task again.

He finished with one side and dropped from the chair to move it to another part of the room and continue putting the lights around.

Aunt Tricia continued in a cheery tone. "What about your mother? How is she? I haven't seen her in a while. I have to visit more often."

"She is doing well. She always wants to have Lucy's pastries, so she gets a lot from the grocery store every day since it's closer to her."

Aunt Tricia nudged Lucy in her side gently and her smile turned mischievous. "It's good to know she is well," she said.

Lucy cleared her throat and ignored the suggestive look in her aunt's eyes. Taylor's compliments always made her flush, but that was probably because it was hard to get one from him. In the past, they had gotten along fine, but since she returned to Ivy Creek after leaving him years back, he had been distant.

Only recently, he had begun talking to her again, and she was thankful they had at least gotten past the anger he felt towards her.

"Let me check on the batter," Aunt Tricia said and headed for the kitchen while Lucy continued to watch Taylor.

"That should do it," Taylor said and dusted his palms together. He jumped down from the chair and landed steadily on his feet. He turned towards Lucy. "Would you need me to do anything else for you?"

Lucy shook her head. "Thank you so much, Taylor," she said.

"Sure."

"You heading back to the station?" Lucy enquired as Taylor slipped his hands into his pockets.

"Heading home," he corrected and pinned his gaze on hers. "I worked all night."

"On Tabitha Alli's case?" she prompted quickly. Lucy had told herself she didn't want to get involved in the case, but she still wanted information. "Have they found the cause of death yet? Does it really have to do with poison?"

"No, we are yet to get the autopsy results, but it might have to do with health issues, so don't get too worked up over it."

A moment of silence passed between them.

"I have to get back home now," he said and patted her shoulder before brushing past her.

"Thanks again for your help," Lucy said and walked with him to the door. They reached for the knob simultaneously, and his hand brushed over hers lightly before she retreated.

The door gave way before either of them could open it, and Richard stood on the other end holding a box and wearing a grin on his face.

"Happy holidays," he announced. "I love what you've done with the place."

The grin disappeared from his face when he looked at Taylor, and Lucy took the box from him. She set it on the floor by her feet and straightened herself again.

"How are you, Richard?" she asked when he entered the bakery and pulled her in for a hug. The embrace lasted a little longer than it usually did, and when he released her, her cheeks flushed red because Taylor still stood by the doorway watching them.

She couldn't read his blank expression, and he turned away before she could try.

"See you around, Lucy," Taylor said and hurried away.

Richard closed the door after him and turned to Lucy again. He extended a hand to push back some strands of hair falling to the side of her face as he asked. "Did you need help with the decorations?"

"Ah yes," Lucy replied, and offered him a shaky smile. She found a chair to sit and offered him one. "Taylor was driving past the bakery, so he stopped and offered to help. There's no way I could have reached the ceiling boards to put up those lights."

She looked up at the decorated part of the ceiling and smiled a little.

"You know, Lucy, you can always reach out to me for help," he said and placed a hand on hers on the table. "I'm always at your beck and call."

Richard winked, and the full-toothed smile he gave her reminded her of his charm. Her insides warmed, and she broke contact to look at the forgotten box on the floor.

"What's in the box?"

"I figured you'd want to do some decorating, so I brought you a box of some stockings and wreath and tinsels I had kept in a box somewhere. And maybe if you're free, you can visit my café to see what I've done with the place."

"I'd like that very much," she replied.

"Me too."

Richard rose to his feet. He leaned in for a peck, taking Lucy by surprise, then he waved at her before heading out of the bakery.

Stunned, Lucy remained seated for some seconds till her aunt came out of the kitchen. "Say nothing," she began before Lucy could muster any words. "I saw everything."

Aunt Tricia's eyes fixed on Lucy's as she added. "I think both of them are into you." Her aunt brought the box to where Lucy sat, put it on the table, and opened it.

Lucy scoffed. "That is crazy," she gasped and covered her cheeks with her hands. Aunt Tricia took out stockings and garlands for their tree.

"Sweet. We didn't have any garlands on the tree," Aunt Tricia said as she emptied the box, then she back-tracked to their former topic again. "Come on, don't tell me you don't see it too, Lucy. Taylor was staring pretty hard when you hugged Richard, and Richard wants you to know you can always ask him for help whenever because Taylor helped you out. I sensed a tiny tinge of jealousy from those words, and with Taylor? Don't even get me started on that look on his face when you hugged Richard. Even a teenager can tell when a guy is into them."

"Taylor and I are a closed chapter, aunty," Lucy said. She ran her hands over her jeans. "And maybe Richard likes me, but it's still early days with him, and I can't really be certain of anything."

Aunt Tricia raised a brow, shooting Lucy a doubting stare.

"I think you're wrong," Lucy continued and stood up to go start her baking for the day. Hannah would be in the bakery soon, and with Aunt Tricia's help, they could get most of the work done before mid-day. She counted what she had to bake in her mind; cupcakes, brownies, and macaroons were on the top of that list.

"If you say so," Aunt Tricia called behind her as they entered the kitchen. "Just be careful not to send mixed signals because I can tell you from experience that that can be very confusing."

Lucy picked up her sieve and walked over to the corner to measure out flour. "Trust me, I won't," she replied as she tied her apron around her neck.

She wasn't interested in Taylor, and with Richard, she had to admit she liked him. Whatever happened, she knew her feelings were as clear as day, so Aunt Tricia had nothing to worry about.

Pushing both men out of her mind, Lucy gathered her thoughts and focused them on the recipes she had in mind for the day.

13

By mid-day, they had finished the baking for the day, and Aunt Tricia had gone home to freshen up and rest a bit. Lucy and Hannah attended to the customers trooping into the bakery at intervals, and they had almost run out of cupcakes.

She took a break and went into the kitchen to get herself a glass of water, and when she returned to the dining area, Hannah was attending to the last customer in front of the counter.

Lucy beamed when she recognized the lady as the one who had suggested the idea of decorating the bakery the last time she was around.

"I love what you've done," the lady said as she handed Hannah cash for her order. "You see that the decorations really give the place the life and vibe it needs for the season."

"You were right," Lucy agreed and they both laughed.

"Although there is one thing missing," the lady continued and looked around the bakery. "Some—"

"Some music," Lucy said before she could complete her sentence. "I know we need some music to lighten the mood. I'm installing a new sound system today, so when next you're here, you'll be rocking back and forth to some festive tunes. You can count on that."

The lady winked at her, got her package from Hannah, and headed for the door just at the same time it opened, and a sales rep from the electronic store walked in.

"Hi." Lucy quickly went around the counter to greet the man who offered to install her speakers the previous day.

"This shouldn't take me long to install," the man said as he accepted her handshake. Lucy pointed him towards the shelf where she had the previous speaker, and he excused himself to start work.

She returned to the back of the counter and stood there chatting with Hannah about her experience at the electronic store while the man worked on the installation. It took him a few minutes to get the speaker working, then he asked Lucy to connect her phone through Bluetooth to the device and play a song.

Lucy chose *It's Beginning to Look a Lot like Christmas* from her playlist, and as the soft sounds filled the air, she started tapping her fingers. She turned to Hannah and said, "Truly, music makes all the difference."

"I agree," Hannah said.

The sales rep walked over to the counter where they stood and offered Lucy a card. "Here is a company number in case you need anything else. The system comes with a year warranty, so if it develops a fault that isn't due to damage, you can bring it back."

"Oh, I didn't know that," Lucy said, wondering why the nosy sales guy she encountered yesterday didn't think to mention that part. "Thank you…"

"Jay," he offered.

"Thank you, Jay," she repeated. Then, she reached into the counter for the bag of cupcakes she had packed for him while he worked. "Here is a present for you," she said as she extended the pack.

Jay's lips curved into a smile. "You're very kind. Thank you." He peered into the pack and looked back at her. "I've had some of your cupcakes before, and they are extremely tasty, better than anything I've had around here in a long time."

"Really? Do you come by the bakery?"

"No, no. I get bread from the grocery store most times, and I tasted your cupcakes when I had a work meeting at one of Blue River's conference rooms," he replied. "I knew they were yours because I've seen a few colleagues eat them and they always mention your bakery when asked where they got them from."

Lucy's heart jumped at his disclosure of the referrals. Any news about the success of her business made her glad. It was also another force that propelled her to work harder to improve her recipes.

"I love our company meetings at Blue River, although Tabitha always had a way of ruining the atmosphere by belittling one of her team," he added.

"I've heard," Lucy said, suspending her own self-appraisal for a while. "It's a tragedy what happened to her, anyway. It must have been a shock to her workers and family."

Jay shook his head. "Trust me, it wasn't so much of a devastating blow."

"What do you mean?" Lucy said as she leaned on her counter.

"I heard a rumor that the staff was celebrating when they heard of her death. Some of them attended the church's award night and they didn't look so distraught. I don't mean to speak ill of the dead, but honesty, I believe her passing will make Blue River do better."

Lucy pondered on his words as he spoke, and once again the feeling of suspicion she felt yesterday concerning Tabitha's demise returned.

It seems more likely that there is someone who must have gone the extra mile to get Tabitha out of the way.

So far, besides Justin Alli, Lucy hadn't spoken to anyone who was a Tabitha fan. The woman seemed to have stepped on a lot of toes, and Lucy imagined what it would be like for Justin, knowing that a lot of the locals didn't like his wife.

He is such a nice man; she thought. A thorny knot of emotion welled up inside her, and she expressed her pity for Justin out loud.

"Still, her husband must be devastated from the shock. I mean, who would benefit from her death?"

"Who wouldn't?" Jay replied, shaking his head. The sarcasm in his words sent a shiver down her spine, and a knot formed in the pit of her stomach when Jay added. "Every single worker at Blue River will benefit from Tabitha's death. That's the reality of it."

Jay thanked Lucy for the cupcakes again before leaving the bakery, and Lucy chewed on her lower lip as Hannah commented beside her. "Well, Tabitha sure had a lot of enemies."

"It sure seems that way," Lucy responded and went back to attending to her customers when another set trooped in.

14

Every single worker at Blue River will benefit from Tabitha's death.

Jay's words rang in Lucy's mind hours after he had left her bakery. She was lost in thought where she sat behind the counter, wondering what he meant by his statement when Hannah suddenly tugged at her arm and dragged her out of her contemplations.

"Look," Hannah said in an excited tone, and Lucy followed the direction of her finger to see an old couple swaying lightly to the song playing.

Santa Claus is Coming to Town played over the speakers, and Lucy realized she had lost track of what was happening in the bakery completely.

"They look beautiful," Hannah complimented as they watched.

Other customers in the bakery also watched the dance the couple performed and when they neared the end, a few others stood up to join them while the rest cheered.

The couple reminded Lucy of her parents, and for a while, she thought of them. Her mother used to dance a lot when she worked in the bakery. There was always a song playing in the background, and it made Lucy enjoy singing and dancing herself.

She remembered during Christmas when she was in high school, they would hang decorations on a tree, and her parents would go shopping for presents, wrap them and place them under the tree at midnight.

Lucy was an only child, so most times she had friends over for Christmas sleepovers. In the mornings, her mother prepared lots of food—roasted potatoes, brussel sprouts, and marinated turkey with stuffing. This had always been her favorite time of the year.

A lump had formed in Lucy's throat as she watched the dancing couple, and her chest tightened with emotion.

I miss you so much, mom and dad...

A tear slipped down her cheeks at the thought, and she laughed it off as she wiped it away with her thumb. She took a deep breath and pressed her fingertips to her eyelids to keep the rest of her tears at bay.

Her heart beat furiously against her chest as she thought of her parents, and she realized for the past several months she had been so wrapped up in work and everything else that she hadn't thought of them in a while.

Her mother always loved this time of the year, and Lucy had grown to love it, too. One reason she had kept the bakery open after their death early this year was because she wanted to keep some part of them alive, and right now, watching her customers dance in the bakery, Lucy felt closer to her mother than she had in months because this was exactly how it was around here when she was alive.

The dance had ended, and everyone returned to their seats again before Hannah spoke. "I want to get off early today to run some errands for the family. I like to finish Christmas shopping early before everyone else, so I don't make a mistake or forget to get anything."

"Sure, you can get off early," Lucy replied. "We've sold almost everything we have prepared and we need to make more for tomorrow."

"Thanks, Lucy," Hannah said and ran a hand over Lucy's back before heading into the kitchen. Lucy gave the adoring couple one last look again before she lowered herself to her seat and picked up a cooking magazine from the table beside her to flip through.

When Hannah finally left for the day, there was only one customer left in the bakery. Lucy thought of closing early to run some errands herself. Watching the couple dance in her dining area had stirred up old memories in her, and she craved a well-grilled turkey with stuffing for Christmas dinner.

She would have to do some shopping for the bakery anyway, and she could use the time to pick out some items for a home-cooked meal. As she pondered on what to do, she returned the magazine she had been reading to a pile she kept in the drawers under the counter.

Lucy heard the doorbell chime, and she said without looking up. "I'll be with you in a second."

She arranged the stack of magazines properly, making sure they stayed stacked on one another. She closed the drawer and straightened to see Zara Stanmore standing on the other side.

"Hi… sorry, I didn't mean to startle you," Zara said when Lucy sucked in a sharp breath."

"That's fine. I wasn't startled," Lucy replied with a smile.

Zara nodded, smiling back at her as she looked around the bakery. "Would you like something?" Lucy asked when Zara's eyes settled on the display counter.

She still had brownies, cupcakes, and coconut bread in stock for the day, and if she could sell some of these before heading out, then that would be perfect.

"I'd like to try some brownies,' Zara said and looked at her again. "And some of those cupcakes with sprinkles."

"Okay," Lucy affirmed and started working on the order. She added an extra brownie for Zara and packed the cupcakes in a fancy paper bag.

"I love how you've decorated the place for Christmas, and the music just adds a wonderful feel to all of it. Good job, Lucy. You've made this place lovelier than it was."

"I'm glad you like it. My aim is to make my customers fall in love with not just my recipes, but also Sweet Delights."

"I understand, trust me. At Blue River, we could hardly decorate this much without consent from Tabitha. She stifled the joy out of Christmas every time."

Zara took her package from Lucy and continued with a wave of her hand. "At least this year we can finally put some decorations up," she said and rolled her eyes.

"I'm sorry to hear that," Lucy offered, and remembered Jay's words again.

Zara stuffed her order into the tote bag hanging on her shoulder. She leaned into the counter, close enough for Lucy to catch a whiff of her strong perfume scent.

"I came around to offer you a business deal," Zara continued, and Lucy's ears perked with interest. "We are hosting a few conferences this month, and a few of them are for businesses from out of town. I thought our guests would need desserts for their meetings, and I cannot think of a better place to get them than Sweet Delights. I'd like to partner with you for this purpose. We sell your pastries at our hotel and serve them to customers who order treats while reserving our conference halls for their events."

"This is the best news I've heard all day," Lucy squealed. Her heart bounced with the excitement, and she enjoyed Zara's short bubble of laughter.

Her eyes danced as she met Zara's, and she could barely stifle the joy rising inside her.

"When do you propose we start? And do you have a specific list of items you'd like for me to deliver?" Lucy questioned. She was already making mental plans for recipes she could add to the usual cupcakes with sprinkles. She could take things to another level by making her fudgy chocolate cake recipe with whipped cream frosting.

This was a new recipe she was considering bringing in for the new year. A lot of her customers already enjoyed her coffee flavored cake and carrot cake. It was time for a fresh addition to the menu. She could add berries and tarts to the top of each slice to make it classy and reduce the addition of cream to make it healthy.

"We can start immediately," Zara replied, matching Lucy's enthusiasm. "I have a list, but of course, add anything else. You're the expert."

Zara handed her a notepad, and she opened it to check the items on the list. "We can make your first delivery next week to give you time to prepare. We have a conference meeting scheduled next week so that works perfectly.

"Yes, it does," Lucy agreed.

"Great. I'll see you around then. I have to run along now." Zara said, turning around to walk away.

Lucy suddenly remembered Jay's words again.

Every single worker at Blue River will benefit from Tabitha's death. She considered asking Zara about what she thought of the murder and stopped Zara from exiting the bakery without weighing her options properly.

"Zara, wait… can I ask you something?"

Zara spun around; her lips slightly parted. "Sure, you can ask me anything," she replied without hesitation and came back to the counter again.

Is this a good idea? What if my questions cause a rift between us? I just got a brilliant business offer from her and I wouldn't want to jeopardize that by stepping on her toes.

Lucy knew she should have considered all this before calling out to Zara, and now she rocked back on her heels, slightly uncomfortable because of the intent gaze Zara threw in her direction.

It's a bad idea… don't ask.

"Actually, never mind," Lucy said, hoping the nonchalant shrug she threw in Zara's direction would make her disregard her initial request.

15

Lucy's cheeks colored when Zara said, "No, I mind. What was on your mind?" and came closer to the counter.

She eyed Lucy, making her more self-conscious, and Lucy wished she had kept her mouth shut. Lucy finally said, "It was nothing."

"Were you going to ask me what my argument with Justin was about?" Zara probed.

Lucy's eyes widened. "I didn't want to pry, so I changed my mind," she said with an apologetic smile and quivering lips. "I was just curious, and I wanted to know if it had something to do with me, or what happened to Tabitha," she added.

"I saw you drive past while we argued, and I know you must have been wondering because it was right after you left the hotel that day." Zara stopped for a second, and Lucy saw her chest heave as she dragged in a shaky breath. "We were arguing about decorations."

"Decorations?" The argument seemed to be about much more than decorations. She remembered seeing lots of fingers jabbing in the air, animated gestures, and eye rolls, and all of that was for decorations? Lucy was interested in hearing the rest of what Zara had to say, but she played down her curiosity by asking in a light tone. "He didn't want to get the place in a festive mood?"

Zara nodded twice. "Justin always had all these great ideas for what the hotel should look like during the festive season, but every time he brought them up, Tabitha shut them down. She never let him have a say in anything, even though he was much more creative than her. Tabitha was blatantly rude to him, and every staffer at Blue River, and if anything went wrong with her ideas, she blamed it on Justin. She always wanted to take the glory for the good stuff and assign the responsibility for failures to him and others. It was very unfair, and Justin just took all of that quietly, to everyone's surprise."

"That's awful," Lucy replied.

"I know," Zara said after a while. "Over time, I watched Justin retreat into a shell, he never contributed to anything anymore, and that day when I brought up the idea of having decorations in the conference halls and the reception, he shut down the idea without even giving it a second thought.

"I had to remind him we had to make changes and look our best for the customers regardless of everything going on or else we would lose our reputation in town."

Lucy shored her frame on the counter as she listened to Zara speak. The woman had the hotel's best interest at heart, she could tell from the passion in her voice.

"He needs to know that his voice is heard now, and the staff at Blue River looks up to him to lead the way."

"I understand," Lucy said in a quiet voice. "I hope you're not offended that I thought to ask about this. I was just curious about it, and I kind of felt like it had to do with me."

"Of course, no it didn't," Zara corrected. "I'm sorry if it came off like I was being rude to Justin on my end, but it was nothing of the sort. Trust me."

Zara put a hand over Lucy's and her lips curled into a smile. "You shouldn't worry about that. We ended up settling for some acceptable ideas for the decorations and we will put them up soon. All you have to focus on is delivering on those treats."

Zara's phone beeped, and she took it out of her pocket. Her brows furrowed a bit as she read the text on the screen before she looked at Lucy again. "I have to go now," she said, backing away from the counter. "Is sometime later this week okay to bring some sample treats over to Blue River?"

"Yes, it is," Lucy replied, and waved at Lucy as she pulled the door open.

Aunt Tricia stood on the other side when the door opened, and Lucy saw her jaw drop when she saw Zara standing there.

"Hey."

"Hi..." Zara replied.

"Wow, you look extremely familiar," Aunt Tricia continued when Zara sidestepped to let her into the bakery. "You don't know me, do you?"

"No, I don't," Zara replied. She glanced at Lucy again, waved, and hurried out of the bakery while Aunt Tricia stared after her.

"Still trying to figure out where you know her from?" Lucy asked.

"Yes… I just can't place the face and I am always good with faces."

"Well, that was Zara Stanmore. She works at Blue River Hotel, and she came here to offer me a contract," Lucy announced, unable to keep her excitement to herself.

"Blue River? Isn't that Tabitha's hotel?"

"Yes. Yes, it is," she responded. Aunt Tricia took a seat and Lucy joined her after she took off the apron and cap she had on.

She sat down and started reading out the items on the list Zara gave her. "Brownies, red velvet cupcakes with frosting and sprinkles, dark-chocolate slices, macaroons, cinnamon rolls, and muffins."

"That's a lot," Aunt Tricia commented and readjusted in her chair. "I think you should be careful with whatever dealings you have with Blue River, Lucy."

"Did something happen?"

"No, not yet. But Blue River staff are still being investigated for Tabitha's sudden death and we want nothing linking you to them," she warned, reminding Lucy of her self-advice to stay out of this case in every way.

16

Lucy entered the conference room the receptionist had directed her to, and she dropped the basket of pastries she came with on the table, adjusted her blue chiffon blouse, and ran her hands over her skirt.

She was never nervous in presentations like this. When she worked in the city, she had interviews from time to time and featured popular restaurants and bakeries in the column she wrote. As a food critic, Lucy had mingled with several high-profile personalities in the culinary world to feel at ease making a presentation.

That life seemed like a long time ago, even though it was only earlier that year that she had returned to her home in Ivy Creek. Alone in the conference room, while waiting for Zara, she wandered to the large window and stood close to it.

The conference room was at the back side of Blue River, and from there, she had a good view of the flat-grass-covered plains.

She saw birds soaring in the sky above a tall tree in the distance, and she admired the clear blue sky. Lucy took off the shawl wrapped around her neck and folded it into her bag. When she left the bakery that morning, the weather was frosty, but now the sun had fully risen. She glanced at the watch on her left wrist and tucked a loose strand of hair behind her ear.

The door swung open then, and Lucy spun around to see Justin step into the room.

"Hi," she breathed out, surprised he was there instead of Zara. "How are you doing?" she asked when he greeted her with a smile. "I'm here to see Zara. We set an appointment for me to deliver some pastries."

"I know," Justin said. "Zara and I talked about it; she couldn't make it in today, so she asked me to do this."

"Oh, great then," Lucy remarked. She clapped her hands together and moved closer to the table to remove the napkin covering the wrapped pastries in the basket. "I brought some of everything she asked for, and you can share some with the other staff once we finish here," she suggested.

"That's very nice of you, Lucy," Justin said.

Lucy took out the cupcakes first for him to try. She watched gingerly as he took a bite and closed his eyes as he chewed.

"Hmmm... amazing," he groaned and took another bite.

Her spirits lifted, and she waited till he dropped the cupcake before trying the muffins next.

The look of satisfaction on his face was the same when he tried the brownies and the macaroons.

Finally, Justin sighed. "I can't seem to make a choice. They all taste amazing to me, and if it were up to me, I'd have you bring us all of them," he said.

Lucy joined in his nervous laugh, and he wiped his lips with the small napkin she handed him.

"But it's not up to me," he added when they became serious again. "I think I should get a chef to come in and taste some of these heavenly treats and make a professional assessment," he said. "If you don't mind, I mean."

"Oh, I don't mind at all," Lucy said confidently. She was a food critic and tasting people's cooking was how she made money for years before she joined the bakery business this year. There was no kind of critical review she hadn't dished out before.

Some of that cynicism from being a critic made her strive to make sure her recipes were perfect.

"Cool, I'll be right back."

Justin left her in the conference room again, and this time she pulled out a chair from the row arranged by the long, boat-shaped table. Justin had left a book on the table when he left, and the picture in front of the notepad caught Lucy's attention.

She took it and looked at the photograph of Justin and Tabitha in front. She guessed it was a pre-wedding photo from how they were dressed, and the back design had a ring by the side of it to confirm that it was.

They looked so young in the picture, and it made her wonder how long they had been married.

Did Justin have to put up with Tabitha, belittling him for a long time? Did they have any kids from their marriage?

Lucy opened the notepad and read the words written on the first page. She realized it was a eulogy for his wife's funeral when she read the first line, and her heart cinched a little towards him.

Dear Tabitha,

Many of us gathered here today did not know you well. To some, you were a neighbor, to others a friend, and a boss... a leader and a teacher, an enemy and a friend, but to me, you were my best friend.

The love of my life.

It saddens me greatly that I have to stand here today to speak about you in front of all these people when I always imagined that you would be with me for many years.

It hurts me you're gone, but somehow it also makes my heart rejoice because your going has freed me from the cage I have lived in all these years.

He crossed the last line of the words Lucy had just read. She stopped reading after that line. She quickly closed the book and pushed it back to the spot where it had been.

Why would Justin write such words to read in front of those many people at his late wife's funeral?

Lucy licked her lips and tried to compose herself as her mind raced with unanswered questions. She didn't want it to be obvious she had been snooping when Justin returned, so she had to act normal.

The door opened as she chided herself about what to do, and Justin came into the room. Reggie, the worker she had met in the electronic store, stepped in after him, and Lucy rose to her feet.

"Sorry I took some time. I had to find Reggie, our assistant chef, to come taste what you've brought. Reggie, this is Lucy, by the way. She owns the bakery Sweet Delights, and we are looking to hire her to supply our hotel with some treats."

Reggie simply nodded his head. He stood behind Justin with a blank look on his face, and Lucy smiled at him, expecting him to acknowledge her presence with a smile or warm greeting.

She cleared her throat when he did neither of those things, and Justin waved a hand at the basket and said, "Shall we?"

"Of course," Lucy replied and took out the first pastry to hand over to Reggie. All the time, she couldn't stop thinking. *What if Justin had the most to benefit from his wife's death over anyone else?*

17

Lucy shifted on her feet as an awkward silence settled in the room.

"Your suggestion at the electronic store was really helpful by the way. The speaker is top-notch, and it serves my needs at the bakery perfectly," Lucy said.

"You two have met?" Justin asked, looking from Reggie to Lucy.

"Yes."

"No," Reggie said.

Lucy's brow perked, and she saw a flash of confusion in Justin's eyes as he looked at both again. "We met once at an electronic store nearby," Lucy explained.

Justin turned to Reggie, whose ears had reddened, and Lucy pressed her lips together. She sensed Reggie did not want Justin to know they had met before, and it made her wonder why.

Did it have something to do with what Reggie told her the last time?

"Well, let's get to tasting," Justin broke into the silence. He cleared his throat and pushed back a chair to sit and watched Reggie lift the muffin to take a bite.

After the muffins, Reggie tasted the cupcakes, then the brownies, and everything else. Lucy linked her fingers together in front of her and waited for his remarks while Reggie took his time to wipe his lips clean before he faced her.

"They all taste wonderful," he said. "This is baking at its finest and I think Zara would love them."

"Thanks," Lucy breathed, feeling relieved that she got a compliment from a fellow chef. She was still grinning when Justin rose to his feet again.

"That settles it then," Justin said and adjusted the sleeve of his shirt.

"I will speak with Zara and come by your bakery with some paperwork to complete our business deal together, then you can start working on your first delivery," Reggie said.

"All right—" Lucy started.

"You should get back to what you were doing before I called you," Justin cut in, looking at Reggie with a straight face, before Lucy could complete her sentence.

She was going to say she looked forward to having Reggie come by her bakery, but she kept that to herself.

Reggie hesitated, but he backed away from the table and headed out of the conference room without another word. A second of silence passed between Justin and Lucy before she smoothed a hand over her skirt and said with a laugh. "So, I'll be expecting you then."

"Yes, I might drop by today or tomorrow," Justin replied.

"Cool."

She gathered the pastry wraps together and folded them inside her napkin before pushing the basket to Justin. "Here, for the rest of your workers."

"Thank you, Lucy. I'll see you when I drop by," he said with a pleasant smile, and picked up the basket.

His gaze dropped on his book on the table, and she saw his brows crease when he said. "I had a pen here."

Lucy's breath hitched in her throat, and her eyes darted across the table. She saw the pen at the side of the table where she sat, and she picked it up to hand it over to him.

She shivered as he took the pen from her, but his frown stayed.

"That's weird. Could have sworn I kept it all together," he murmured and pressed the ball of the pen. "See you around, Lucy," he said one last time before he left the conference room.

Lucy stood in the same spot for some seconds, and when she finally exited the room, she prayed silently that Justin did not suspect someone had messed with his things on the table.

She didn't want him to suspect that she knew about his eulogy.

18

Lucy hurried to her car and was glad when she shut the door behind her. She ran her hands through her hair and let out a deep sigh as she remembered the trepidation she had felt as Justin assessed his belongings before he left the room.

She closed her eyes, let out a deep breath, and opened them again to hear her phone ping in her purse. When she entered the hotel, she had forgotten her purse in her car.

Had it been pinging the entire time?

After a brief search, Lucy retrieved her phone from the purse. She saw the text message banner on the screen with the name Richard, and a smile crossed her lips when she opened them and read.

Hey, Lucy, up for a date tonight? If yes, respond with a cute emoji.

Shaking her head, she responded to the text and waited till it double ticked.

Richard replied immediately, and she grinned harder as she read his reply.

Sweet! Pick you up by seven. I can't wait.

Lucy drove back to the bakery after that. Hannah was in charge whenever she was away, and when Lucy returned, the place was swamped with customers. A traditional Christmas carol played from the speakers, and she joined Hannah in serving, putting in additional cupcakes for every customer who ordered.

It seemed like a lot to give to every customer, but Lucy followed her mother's business rules of generosity. Customers loved the attention given to them when they entered a place. No one would return to a place with subpar service, and she had to make sure she stayed on top of her game with the customers here in Ivy Creek. They could be easy to satisfy and difficult to please all at once.

"Have a nice day," Lucy said to the last customer she served. The woman tipped her a five-dollar bill before walking away, and she turned to Hannah.

"So how did it go with Justin Alli?" Hannah asked as she took off the apron tied to her body.

"Went well," Lucy replied. "He will drop by for us to complete some paperwork and I am to deliver my first batch next week."

"This is amazing news, definitely worth celebrating." Hannah strolled into the kitchen and returned with a bottle of grape juice. She waved the bottle at Lucy and continued in a singing voice. "How about a little juice to celebrate your success so far?"

"I'll have to use your offer now because I've got a date at seven," Lucy said.

"Let me guess, Richard?"

Before Lucy could say anything, Hannah raised her hand to signify Lucy didn't have to say anything and went into the kitchen to bring two glasses. Both ladies sat in the empty dining area to enjoy the grape juice with a slice of cake for themselves.

"Yes, he's picking me up."

"That's nice," Hannah commented as she took a sip. "I have a date myself, but over the weekend."

Lucy lifted her glass for a toast. "To a Merry Christmas and an amazing forthcoming new year."

She clinked her glass against Hannah's before they continued drinking.

When they finished their mini celebration, they continued work. It was past six when Lucy and Hannah finally closed the bakery for the day and Lucy raced up the stairs to get ready for her date.

She breezed through the clothes in her closet to find something suitable to wear and ended up settling for a black long-sleeved dress with a V-neck cut and length that stopped over her knees.

Lucy paired it with knee-high boots and wrapped a shawl around her neck for extra comfort and to protect herself from the cold. She finished dressing and stood in front of her mirror, admiring her reflection, when Gigi pranced towards her.

"Hey, Gigi," she called, bent over, and scooped the cat in her arms. "You look pretty. Do I look pretty too?"

Gigi purred, and she stroked its head. Lucy developed second thoughts about the dress as she continued to stare at herself in the mirror.

Do I look too serious? Maybe I should add more lip-gloss, or lipstick to outline my lips.

Her cheeks reddened when she caught herself wondering if Richard preferred a woman with natural looks or a bit of make-up.

Come on, Lucy, get a grip.

She pressed her free hand to her cheek and exhaled before looking at Gigi again. A honk from outside told her Richard had arrived, and she checked the clock on the wall and noticed that he was right on schedule.

Lucy set Gigi carefully on the floor, grabbed her purse, and smoothed a hand over her hair one last time before she headed out of her apartment.

Richard was at the door when she opened it, and he wore a wide smile. His brown eyes danced as his gaze trailed over her. "You look so beautiful," he whispered.

Heat filled her insides again when Richard stepped closer and kissed her cheeks. "Tonight is all about fun," he added, linked their fingers, and led her towards his black sedan.

Seconds later, they were driving down the high street towards the bend that led downtown.

———

They strolled into the restaurant Richard picked for their dinner date, and Lucy matched his steps until they got to their reserved table. She sat with him and picked up the menu to make an order, all the while aware of Richard's stare.

She met his eyes when her attention shifted from the menu, and she smiled at him.

"I'll have the bacon and cheese croquettes," she ordered.

"Same with the lady," Richard said and closed his menu. The waiter returned with their wine first, and two glasses, and they indulged in that while waiting for their starters.

Lucy put down her glass after she had taken another sip and looked around the restaurant. The décor was cozy and had a European feel about it. Everything seemed perfect in a very understated way, which she liked.

"How did you find this place?" she asked, looking around again.

"It's very popular in town," Richard replied. "They have the best steak here, and they are well known for serving the best wine." He tipped his glass in her direction.

Lucy glanced over her shoulder at the area near the entrance. She gasped when her gaze zeroed in on Taylor. He sat opposite a blonde woman, his gaze glued to her face, and from where Lucy sat, she saw his magnificent smile widen before he brushed his hand against hers.

Heat rose to the back of her neck, and she quickly averted her gaze.

"Hey, you with me?" Richard was saying. "Have you heard a thing I said in the past second?"

"Ahh, yes," she lied and covered her shock with a smile. "I was just admiring the scenery. This is a really lovely place."

"What were you looking at exactly?" he probed and scanned the area before looking at her.

She pretended to cough to command his attention, and she was glad when he focused his gaze on her. Lucy placed a hand on his, but before she could think of what to say next, the waiter arrived with a tray.

He set it in front of them, and she picked up a napkin, laid it on her lap, and smiled at Richard again. As she took the first bite of her starter, she cast another glance over her shoulder toward where Taylor sat.

Taylor rose to his feet as she stared, and placed his hand at his partner's waist, leaned into her and whispered something before smiling again.

Lucy rolled her eyes and turned away. She hadn't seen him smile at her like that since she returned to Ivy Creek, and she couldn't believe that he was having a good time here with another woman.

Who was the blonde, anyway? She wondered as she redirected her focus to her meal.

19

The next morning, Hannah arrived early. Lucy couldn't go back to sleep when she was woken up by a noisy truck that went past her building at four am, so she had spent the early hours of the morning in the kitchen baking.

She had cupcakes and brownies ready when Hannah arrived, and she started on the macaroons and muffins for the day. It was a Saturday morning, and the wintry air was a pleasant excuse for Lucy to wear a new sweatshirt to keep the cold away. She stepped away from the center table to wash her hands.

Hannah turned to her. "How did it go with Richard last night?" she asked. Hannah turned on the electric whisker and watched it beat the eggs she already set in the bowl.

"The restaurant we went to was amazing, and their chicken thighs are the best I've ever tasted."

"Really? What's the name?"

"Rossdale," Lucy replied, then she described the lighting and the beautiful scenery inside. "From the outside, it looks like some random restaurant, but inside is beautiful and the service is spectacular. You should try it sometime when you've got the chance, maybe for your date," Lucy said.

"Yeah right."

"You still haven't told me who it is," Lucy continued.

Hannah turned off the whisker. "What did you two do after dinner?" she asked, steering the conversation away from her again.

Lucy shot her a knowing smile but allowed it to slide. She mentioned her drive around town with Richard after, and their stop by an ice cream parlor for some ice cream before he brought her back home.

"I also ran into Taylor with some blonde woman at the restaurant. He didn't see me, and he left not too long after I spotted him."

"Oh," Hannah said and dropped what she was doing.

Lucy shrugged. "He seemed like he was having fun…" she continued, but trailed off and looked at Hannah, who already shot her an amused look.

"You sound like there's a but."

"There's no but," she said, dismissing thoughts of who the woman with Taylor was.

It's not your business, Lucy.

"So why do you sound disappointed that he was having fun with someone else?"

"I do not," she said in a high-pitched tone that made Hannah raise a brow and laugh. "I do not sound disappointed, trust me," she added.

Hannah shrugged. "If you say so."

"I say so."

They returned to work quietly and finished the baking in time to open the bakery for the day. It was almost mid-day when Pastor Evans walked into the bakery, and Lucy welcomed him with a smile. He was dressed in a plain black t-shirt and jeans, and his brown hair was neatly swept away from his face.

She hadn't seen him since the incident at the church, and she suspected he also hadn't dropped by because he was probably swamped with police investigations and dealing with the spooked town members.

"How are you doing, Lucy?" he asked when he reached the counter. "I'm so sorry. I haven't come around here to thank you for the treats you brought to the church the last time. I really appreciate your contribution."

"It's all right," she responded. "How have you been? And how is your wife, Sarah?"

"We are both fine. I would like some macaroons and a loaf of bread, please," he ordered. "Add some brownies to that."

Lucy took care of the order and asked when she handed him the package. "I was wondering, when is the funeral taking place?"

"In a few days," he replied and handed his card over for payment. "We've been waiting for some information from the family and that's now been sorted."

Lucy nodded. "It's a tragedy what happened," she said.

"Indeed."

She remembered Justin's words in his eulogy, and it prompted her next question. "Did they get along? Justin and Tabitha, I mean. Did they get along well as a couple?"

Pastor Evans looked up at the ceiling and rubbed his chin. "They were just like every other couple, you know. Every relationship has its difficulties, and so did theirs. They never had an issue they couldn't work through."

"I understand," Lucy responded in a low tone. "It must be so hard for Justin right now to navigate through his hurt."

"I should head back home, Lucy. Have a nice day," he said and waved at her. She watched him walk out of the bakery, and Zara entered immediately as he left.

"Lucy," she called with enthusiasm and strode to the counter. "I'm sorry you didn't see me the last time you came around. I had a lot on my plate, and I had to attend a business meeting."

"A business meeting?" she asked, walking around the counter to come sit with Zara, who had helped herself to a chair. "I thought you were the head chef at the hotel."

"I was." Zara moved her head from side to side and announced with a bouncing grin. "Justin promoted me to operations director because I have good ideas for Blue River and he made someone else head chef."

"I see," Lucy murmured.

"He made Reggie head chef, and he told me you two met when you came by."

"Yes, we did," Lucy replied. "He tasted the pastries I brought over and liked them. Are you here to deliver the paperwork?"

"No, silly," Zara replied and slapped Lucy's arm playfully. "I am here to say hello, and to get some of those amazing cupcakes of yours."

Lucy went over to the counter and returned with two cupcakes for Zara on a plate.

"They always taste amazing, and I'm going to enjoy having these served at Blue River," she said as she took a bite.

"Me too," Lucy said.

Zara left the bakery when she finished the cupcakes and Hannah joined Lucy in the dining area when they were alone again.

"This is a wonderful offer," Hannah said. "We have a lot to benefit from this deal."

"I know," Lucy said. She didn't doubt that it was, but after her last meeting with Justin, there was this twist in her gut that made her think—what if something went wrong?

"I hope it all goes according to plan," Lucy said and stood up from her chair to get back to work. If it did, then this would only be the beginning of greater things.

20

Since the holidays began, Lucy had barely had time to visit her concession stand at the park. On Saturday morning, she drove there to spend some time and inspect sales while Hannah stayed at the bakery with Aunt Tricia.

The park was full of people; families and kids running around, trying to build and recreate holiday memories.

"How's it going?" Lucy asked Dana, the lady employed to keep the concession stand running. "Lots of sales?"

"Yes... but not as much as it used to be anyway," she replied with a smile as she packed up a muffin for a girl in line. "It's winter. Not so many people hang out here when it snows."

Lucy snuggled into the fluffy coat she wore and adjusted the hoodie on her head. "That's fine. We can change the closing hours till winter's over. Does that sound good?"

Dana replied with a gentle nod and a smile that Lucy acknowledged before she turned around to examine her surroundings. She noticed a man sitting on the street bench not far off from where she stood. He got up and walked away, heading toward the park's exit. Lucy realized he had left a notepad behind on the chair when she went closer to the bench to sit and relax a little.

She picked it up and chased after the man without hesitating. When she got up to him, she tugged on his winter jacket as he turned around.

"You forgot your... Justin," she said when he looked at her. "I didn't realize it was you," she said and swallowed. "You left this behind."

He took the notepad from her. "Thanks Lucy, I didn't even notice I didn't have it with me."

"No problem."

Lucy propped her hands on her hips, and he eyed her a little.

"How are you?"

"I'm great, you?"

"I'm all right. Just thought I could sit here for a while and enjoy the view," he said.

"It actually is a lovely view."

They looked around, and faced each other again, Lucy wondering why Justin was staring at her.

"Are you in a hurry?" he asked. "I'd like to sit with you for a while, if that's all right."

"That's fine," Lucy agreed.

They walked back to the bench, and she adjusted the gloves on her hand. She sat with him on the bench and noticed he still wore his wedding ring when he placed his hands on his lap.

Lucy raised her gaze and met Justin's, and he gave her a smile that didn't reach his eyes. His shoulders sloped, sagging his body down, and he exhaled as if trying to get some load off his chest.

"I saw Zara yesterday," Lucy said, attempting to start a conversation that would ease the awkward silence.

Justin picked up on that and continued. "That's good. I recently promoted her, so she has been really busy running around getting things together. She is an active woman and very business-minded."

"I know," Lucy said. "She mentioned Reggie bringing over some paperwork within the next week before I make the first delivery."

Justin nodded again. "True. I just want to see everything move along smoothly and quickly, and it seems like I am under a lot of pressure from myself to do all of that."

He stopped and ran a hand through his hair. "Tabitha always handled all the business stuff, and since her passing, I've been trying to navigate through it alone. It's been quite difficult."

"I'm so sorry for your loss, Justin," Lucy said. "I heard about the funeral; Pastor Evans mentioned it the last time he was at my bakery."

"You'll be there, right?" Justin asked.

She hesitated. "I don't know."

"I'd like for you to be there, Lucy," he said.

A lump formed in Lucy's throat. She swallowed to push it down, but it stayed when she saw Justin's eyes water.

"Tabitha was a very passionate woman, despite her faults. She loved her business, she loved this town, and I just feel as if… most of the people here don't know this side of her, so I don't think I will get much sympathy on that day. It's not news to me that my wife lacked fans even within her inner circle."

"I think you'll hang in there just fine, Justin," Lucy said. She touched his hand and squeezed it to show her support, and he sighed again.

"My staff are doing their best to keep the place running, just like it used to when she was with us. They all work very hard, especially Zara. She deserved the promotion. It also seems like some of them have blossomed in her absence. At least I can say business is better than it used to be."

Lucy kept her hand on his and she saw him look down at it. "I would really appreciate it if you showed up for the funeral."

Lucy's throat was too tight for her to speak properly, so she nodded twice before saying, "I'll do my best."

"Thanks for sitting with me, Lucy," he said and pulled away from her. "I need to get back to work."

She waved at him and relaxed on the bench, letting her back rest on it. She turned when someone called her name and saw Taylor standing beside her.

He sat when she straightened up on the bench, and Lucy faced him. "Hey, what's going on? What are you doing around here?" she asked.

"I came to check on someone across the street and I saw you here," he replied. His gaze flickered over her face for a second and rested on her eyes.

"Work related?"

"Yes," he said. "I saw you with Justin, and I came to say hello."

"Oh, that... we were just talking about the funeral and some business arrangement," she replied with a dismissive wave of her hand.

"You're in business with Justin?" he asked.

The ridge of Lucy's back went straight. "You sound like that's a crime," she said when she heard the tinge of suspicion in his voice.

"No, it's not, it's just..." his voice trailed off, and he rubbed his jaw. "We have our eyes on Blue River, and it's best you are careful with your association with them for the time being. At least till everything blows over."

"I know that. Trust me, you don't have to tell me."

"Good."

She saw a smile wrinkle up his lips after a second, and he chuckled.

"What?"

"Nothing. This reminds me of when we were in high school. This park, and winter. We used to come here a lot when it snowed, and we had that spot under that tree," he said and pointed at an oak tree. A couple sat on the bench under its wide branches and the image of them reminded Lucy of the time Taylor spoke about. Back then, she enjoyed coming here with Taylor during summer and every time she had free time on her hands.

They had shared their first kiss at that same spot. Lucy's cheeks flamed when the memory came to her, and she hoped he didn't see her blush.

"It used to be so much fun," she agreed and chuckled. When she quieted down again, she looked at him. "You know, I saw you at that posh restaurant called Rossdale downtown two days ago with some hot blonde."

"Really?" Taylor asked, amused. "I didn't see you. Were you with someone?"

"Yeah," she replied. "Who were you with?"

Lucy found her heart was thudding in her chest as she waited for his reply. *Was she his new girlfriend? A colleague? Or neighbor?*

"She's a new friend," he replied after assessing her for a while. She noticed a mischievous twinkle in his eyes. "What about you? Who were you with it?"

"Richard Lester," Lucy replied and saw his lips turn downward.

Taylor averted his eyes from hers, and shifted on the chair, leaning farther away from her. She saw his jaw muscle firm into a rigid line, and he stood up.

"Make sure you're careful in whatever business you have with anyone affiliated with Blue River," he said and stormed away, leaving Lucy confused.

She didn't understand what made him angry suddenly, and she battled with trying to figure it out the entire ride back to her bakery.

21

The bakery boomed with activity by the time Lucy returned, and she dove right in, serving customers, accepting tips, and sending them off with smiles and well wishes for the holidays.

Hannah came out of the kitchen with a tray of brownies, and she displayed them on the counter, taking her time to make sure they were properly arranged on the tray. Aunt Tricia conversed with some older men who came in together to get their fill of carrot cake, and Lucy smiled when she saw her aunty slip one of them an extra cupcake.

She shook her head and turned to Hannah. "Do you see how Aunt Tricia lights up with those men? It reminds me of when I used to watch my parents talk. They always tried to iron things out between them without an argument."

"That sounds cute." Hannah closed the counter and set down the tray she held. "My parents argue a lot, but it's always worth it in the end because they settle their differences and understand each other better after that."

"My dad hated confrontation," Lucy continued wistfully. Recently, she thought of her parents a lot, and the tug in her heart whenever those thoughts came reminded her of how much she missed them. "My mom knew that, so she tried her best to speak to him without sounding judgy. I didn't know much back then, but I admire what they had."

Hannah put a hand on Lucy's shoulder. "Don't worry, you'll get it," she said and laughed as she walked into the kitchen.

No customer was waiting to be served, so Lucy took a break and followed Hannah into the kitchen to continue their discussion. "Don't read meaning into this… I just miss my parents, that's all. I'm not longing for marriage or babies yet or anything."

"I know," Hannah pointed out in a melodious voice. She tipped the ladle she held in Lucy's direction and continued. "I just think you miss them this much because you're always alone, and you only go out when Richard invites you to. Do something fun alone… I thought that was the idea of this entire blonde thing."

Hannah made a gesture towards Lucy's hair, and Lucy touched a strand.

"My roots are getting darker again. I might need a touch-up soon."

"Yeah, but that's not my point. My point was you should go out more and have some fun. For example, I have an art function tonight with my sister, and it will be fun."

"Your sister is the date you talked about?" Lucy interjected, and Hannah cleared her throat.

"I might have lied about that date," she said with a shrug. "I just didn't want you to think I wasn't having fun myself this holiday season."

"But you're not." Lucy giggled when she saw the exasperated look on her friend's face, and she chuckled. "I'm kidding. If art's fun for you, then you should go."

Her phone pinged in her pocket, and she took it out as she continued talking. "In fact, if I didn't have an event lined up for tonight myself, then I might have come with you."

"You have an event?"

"Yes, Richard and I planned to visit the cinema together last time we were out, and…" her words died in her throat as she read the text she just received from Richard. "And he just texted me to cancel."

"So, you're free tonight, then?" Hannah picked up their conversation again, this time with more enthusiasm. "This will be so interesting if three of us go together."

"I don't know much about art," Lucy said and searched for a more concrete excuse. "And I should just take this time to work on the recipes we will be delivering to Blue River next week."

Aunt Tricia came into the kitchen then, and she took off the cap over her hair. "I'm leaving Lucy. I have a date."

"What?" Hannah exclaimed in a melodious voice.

Her laugh filled the kitchen, and Aunt Tricia joined her.

"You're the only one who isn't doing anything fun tonight. Don't you think you should join me?" Hannah urged again.

Lucy rubbed the back of her neck and tried to decide, but in the end, she shook her head. "I should stay back and work on the recipes, but you should have fun."

She faced her aunt. "Enjoy yourself, Aunt Tricia."

"I sure will, honey," Aunt Tricia replied.

She was waving as she left the kitchen with her bag, and Hannah came over to where Lucy stood. She began taking off her apron and cap, then combed her fingers through her hair to free her blonde tresses.

"I'll see you tomorrow, Lucy."

She hugged Hannah briefly and left. Thirty minutes into working on her recipes and Lucy wished she had gone out with Hannah.

It was so silent inside the bakery that she sat outside on the front porch for a while. At least that way, she could enjoy watching the sunset while working on the recipes.

She finished early, locked her front doors, and turned on the speakers to listen to some Christmas songs while she fixed a quick dinner for herself and Gigi. Lucy usually made sure Gigi stayed upstairs, to avoid her coming into the bakery when she had customers, but tonight, she opened the middle door, and allowed Gigi to come stay with her in the kitchen.

Lucy danced alone while the water for her pasta sizzled, and went around the kitchen, gathering items to prepare some sauce. When she finished preparing her meal, she fixed Gigi a quick one and sat down to eat in silence.

Time dragged slowly, and Lucy read through the modifications she intended to make to her recipes one last time before she cleaned up to retire for the night.

She heard a loud bang on her front door as she locked the kitchen to head upstairs, and she froze in her tracks.

Who could it be?

She wasn't expecting anyone, and so far, she had gotten no calls or texts. Lucy hesitated, not wanting to let anyone in at this time of the night.

The knock came again, followed by a familiar voice calling her name. Lucy let Gigi down from her arms and crossed over to the side window of the bakery.

She saw Zara standing outside from where she stood, and she relaxed a bit before going to open the door.

"Hey, Zara," Lucy said when she opened up.

"Good evening, Lucy," she greeted and adjusted the bag on her shoulder. "Should have come sooner, but I got caught up at work, and I couldn't make it earlier. Can you let me in? Let's go over the deal. I have the paperwork here."

"Right now?"

"We should finalize it before Monday, and I won't have time after now. So yes, right now," she replied, her words ending in a plea.

Lucy sighed and stepped away from the door to let Zara in. She closed the door and latched the lock again. "All right, so what are we looking at?"

22

Lucy invited her into the kitchen, offered her a glass of water and a seat, then poured herself a glass of water before she sat.

"Here are the documents for you to sign, and these are special recipes I would like for you to add. We sometimes have special guests who have special diets because of health issues and we have to meet the needs of these VIP guests."

"I understand," Lucy responded as she flipped the pages of the bonded document.

"Your payment and every other detail are written there, so take your time and go through it."

Zara sipped from her glass, and Lucy adjusted herself on her chair as she read the pages. She felt Zara's gaze on her the entire time, and it almost made her squirm.

Zara Stanmore had intense dark eyes. It made Lucy wonder if anyone had ever told her how disconcerting they made people feel when she looked at them. Or was she just being overly sensitive?

She finally got to the last page after minutes of reading the document and looked at Zara. "I will have to get a pen."

She went to the counter where she kept her notepad to get a pen and when she looked back, Zara had left her chair. Zara stood by the counter where Lucy kept some dry ingredients for her baking, and she pointed. "Wild cats?" she asked.

Zara pointed at the sticker on the counter and asked again. "You attended University of Arizona?"

"Yeah, my mother went there," Lucy replied. "She talked about the school a lot. Did you go there too?"

Zara nodded. "I grew up in Arizona with my parents… My mom, actually, because my father left when I was six. He moved far away, so I never got to see him much, at least not till I lost my mother."

"I'm so sorry to hear that," Lucy said. She sat down again and signed the document and closed the file.

Zara shrugged. "Thanks. When she died, I moved away and finally settled here. Seeing this sticker just reminded me of what my life was like those many years ago in Arizona, you know. Your childhood is one time of your life you can never forget if you know what I mean."

"Oh, I know what you mean," Lucy replied sincerely. Her decision to stay back in Ivy Creek after her parents' funeral earlier that year made her realize how much she had missed home, and Lucy had learned to be grateful for support from family and friends since she returned.

"Ivy Creek helped me discover my passion for hospitality and cooking, and also helped me grow my career, so I don't regret moving here at all," Zara said. "Working at Blue River helped me grow my skill too."

"But it must have been so hard working for Justin and Tabitha, right? Considering how Tabitha treated her staff and how Justin could never stand up to her."

The smile on Zara's face faded in the blink of an eye. "That has nothing to do with Justin," she snapped. "Don't you dare talk about him that way."

"I'm sorry, I didn't mean to upset you, I just—"

"Stop talking!" Zara raised a hand to hush her, and she took a step towards Lucy. "Justin has done nothing wrong. He is a victim of everything that happened."

Lucy's stomach churned when Zara's face paled, and she averted her gaze.

"My God, what's wrong with me?" Zara said in a broken voice and tendered Lucy an apologetic smile as if she hadn't just snapped moments ago. "I'm so sorry. I didn't mean to snap like that. I guess I'm just tired from a long day at work, and my nerves are a bit on edge."

Lucy took in a long, shallow breath. "Its fine," she said with a nervous laugh to ease the tension that hung in the air moments earlier.

"When you work with people for a long time, they become family to you, and it's only natural that I would defend my family like that," Zara said as she started to pace the kitchen. She raked her hand through her hair and stopped again when Lucy straightened up.

"I mean, if anyone talked about my father in a certain way, or my mother, then I would also react the way you did. It's normal to defend the people you care about," Lucy said.

Zara froze in her steps and shot Lucy an unflinching look. Her pupils dilated, and she dropped her hands to her side. The cold look in her eyes sent a chill down Lucy's spine, and a wave of nausea reached her as it suddenly dawned on her.

Was it possible? What were the chances that Justin was Zara's father?

Lucy's entire system pumped with adrenaline as she asked in a shaky voice.

"Is Justin your father?" Lucy blurted.

She gasped when Zara nodded in affirmation, and her knees nearly gave way. "I came out here because of him. After my mother passed away, I had no one else, and I thought I should find him, but he... he had forgotten all about his daughter, and he couldn't even recognize me. I don't blame him. He left because my mom wanted him to, but a part of me was still hurt that he didn't even look for me. I wondered for a long time if he loved me at all, and when I met him again after all these years, I realized he did. He just couldn't show it because he wasn't free."

Lucy's stomach churned harder the more Zara talked. "Who else knows about this?" Lucy probed further.

"Tabitha recently found out," Zara replied. She took a step closer to where Lucy sat, and Lucy gripped the edge of the table in front of her so tight, her knuckles turned white. She fought against the cold, paralyzing terror tearing at her insides when Zara's lips curved into a cynical smile.

"She wasn't supposed to find out, but she did. It was my secret to keep, and she couldn't keep out of my business, so I had to do something."

Lucy's head swooned. Her right hand moved to her pocket for her phone, and when she didn't touch anything, she gasped.

"Looking for this?" Zara asked and pointed at the phone on the side counter of the sink.

Oh, sugar... I left it there when I got her a glass of water.

Lucy licked her dry lips and rose to her feet slowly.

"So, you killed her? Because she knew your secret?"

"I didn't want to," Zara said and continued pacing again.

Lucy had moved from where she stood. If she could distract Zara long enough to make it to the door, then she could run upstairs and use the landline in her living room to place a call to the cops. She just had to make sure Zara kept talking.

"I hated the way she treated him. He's my father, and he deserves more than some woman who wouldn't respect him, even in front of strangers. I had to set him free. You get that right?"

Lucy suspected Zara wanted sympathy from her, but how could she look her in the eye and lie? She didn't get it—her heinous act could never be justified. No matter what Tabitha did, Lucy believed Zara had no right to kill her.

She didn't voice out any of these thoughts, instead, she kept her eyes glued to Zara's.

"It must have been hard watching your father every day and knowing he didn't recognize you must have made it worse, but…"

"Are you going to stand there and justify Tabitha?" Zara cut in.

"I'm not doing that; I just don't think that…"

"She deserved what she got," Zara interrupted again. She took three menacing steps towards Lucy who backed away, and Lucy's heart began to pound against her ribcage.

Try to hold still, Lucy… deep breaths. There's always a way out.

The distance between her and Zara was short, and she tried to calculate her options. If she made a run for the door, Zara would get to her before she touched the doorknob. She also couldn't risk staying here with her.

It was nearly ten pm, and no one was coming this way. How could she get out of this situation?

"I could not watch her disrespect him anymore. With her out of the way, he now sees me," she said as she kept coming closer, and Lucy backed towards the wall.

"With her dead, I can finally be happy with my father, and not have to worry about what insults he would get if she ever found us speaking. Everything that went wrong in my family was her fault."

"Zara," Lucy murmured when she got so close. At this point, Lucy could barely breathe without the tightness in her chest closing in on her.

"Now, you know the truth, and you have to go too."

Lucy lunged for the doorknob then and pushed the door open, but she wasn't fast enough. Zara dragged her back, shut the door with a loud bang, and hurled her against it.

She whimpered when her back crashed on the door, pain radiating through her. Zara's hands encircled her neck, shutting her air supply with one squeeze.

"I'm sorry, Lucy, but you have to die."

Lucy fought her off with every bit of her strength. Her nails dug into her wrists and she tried to dislodge Zara's grip, but she failed.

Slowly, her fight faded, and her gaze became blurry. Air stopped getting to her lungs, and she felt her eyes bulge out of their sockets.

Someone help me! She tried to scream but couldn't form any words, not when Zara's tight grip was crushing her windpipe.

Her eyes fluttered, and she gave up, slipping away into the terrifying darkness consuming her. Lucy opened her eyes one last time and stared into Zara's dark eyes. The dreadful smile on her pale face etched into Lucy's memory and she didn't think she could ever get it out.

If this was her last moment on Earth, then she didn't want to go down alone. With the rest of her strength, she jerked her knee forward, bringing it in contact with Zara's pelvic region.

Zara yelped and staggered away from her, giving Lucy time to inhale a large chunk of air. She grabbed the door and dashed into the stairway, shutting the door, and locking it behind her before she hurried to her living room.

She fell on her knees when she got to the living room, her hands shaking as she struggled to get on her feet again and get to the phone. Downstairs, she could hear Zara hitting the door.

It was a wooden door, weakened from years of use, and Lucy knew with the right amount of force it would cave. She got to the phone in time and dialed 911.

"I need help," she said and screamed when Zara's hands closed in on her again.

They wrestled to the ground, Zara staying on top of her. Her hands snaked around Lucy's neck one last time, and she pressed hard.

"It's a shame, Lucy, I liked you," was the last thing Lucy heard before she blacked out.

23

Lucy opened her eyes with a loud gasp, and she struggled to free herself. She fought against the tightness in her throat, wanting to breathe, and she felt warm hands come around her arms.

"It's all right… Lucy, it's me, Tricia, you're safe."

The sure words cut through the terror clouding her brain, and Lucy's fight slowly disseminated. She broke into tears, and the sobs wracked through her body as her aunt's arms came around her body.

"You're safe," Aunt Tricia murmured and consoled her, patting her back and running a hand down her back. "I'm with you.

Her shoulders sagged, and she sank into her aunt's arms, wanting the warmth of her embrace to offer safety.

"I thought I was going to die," she murmured, her voice a bare croak when she could finally speak.

Her throat burned, and she lifted a hand to her neck to feel the soreness.

"I came right on time. Zara had her hands around your neck, strangling you when I arrived, and I stopped her with a bat I found in a corner."

"How did you know to come?" she asked.

"I finished my date and decided to spend the night at your apartment because you were alone. When I came, the doors were locked, but the lights inside were on. I tried calling but couldn't reach you, then I heard the loud crash from upstairs and knew I had to get in," Aunt Tricia explained.

"I was right on time," she repeated. "I remembered you always kept a spare key under the flowerpot on the porch and I used that to let myself in. When I got upstairs, I found you struggling for your life."

"What about Zara?" Lucy asked. She continued forcing herself to take deep, relaxing breaths, and she wanted to ease the wild race her nerves still hadn't recovered from.

"I knocked her out hard, and by the time she regained consciousness, the cops had arrived. They took her away immediately, and just in time, because they were going to search for her at her house."

"They found out she's the killer?"

Aunt Tricia's head bobbed twice. "The autopsy report came back. Turns out she poisoned Tabitha with a strong substance."

"The cops found out?"

"They knew she died from poison, but wanted to investigate where it came from quietly, so they held back the details of the case from everyone. It was a smart move because Zara would have skipped town if she suspected they were onto her."

Lucy remembered Taylor warning her about associating with any staff from Blue River. She sank into the bed, sighed, and closed her eyes.

Her body still ached, and she was feeling dizzy again. "I'm just glad you're safe, Lucy," her aunt said and this time picked her hand up from the bed. "Today is Tabitha's funeral, and I promised Justin I would come on your behalf. He was here to check in on you hours ago."

"Oh," she murmured, already slipping away. Her eyes closed for a second and when she opened them again, a doctor had come into the room.

"I'll be back, honey," Aunt Tricia said when the doctor asked her to leave. "Don't worry about a thing and rest. This Christmas will be filled with many beautiful things, just like you love it."

Aunt Tricia kissed Lucy on the cheek and left the room. The doctor checked the IV connected to her arm and administered an injection that instantly made her drowsy.

"How long will you keep me here" she slurred as the drug took effect.

"Not for long, miss. Don't worry. As soon as we're certain you've passed some tests, you'll be free to go home."

"Good," she whispered and licked her dry lips. "I would hate to spend Christmas here." A smile crept on her lips as she dozed off and for a second, she thought the doctor smiled back at her.

Lucy fell asleep and dreamed of making snow angels in her backyard with her parents. At some point, she heard a deep voice speak to her softly, and her eyes twitched open. She thought she saw Taylor through her hazy vision, but she couldn't be sure.

She went back to sleep for the second time and dreamed of a happy Christmas, full of music and laughter, just like the ones she had in her childhood.

Lucy wanted a Christmas full of laughter and joy, and she hoped she'd get it once she could get this grogginess out of her system.

24

Three days later was Christmas eve, and Lucy was very much in the Christmas spirit the entire day. The bakery emptied early, and all she did since she got up was sing carols and festive songs as she worked.

Now, with Hannah, Aunt Tricia, and Richard, she danced to another tune playing in the background. Richard pulled her close, and they moved slowly to the song while Aunt Tricia went into the kitchen to bring some mulled wine.

They made a toast to the coming year and all the good things they wished would happen in their lives. Lucy was especially thrilled with how things had turned out in her life after her parents' death.

The bakery was doing better than she expected, and she had escaped several brushes with death. She was grateful for all of that.

"To Christmas," Aunt Tricia said after refilling everyone's glass.

They clinked and cheered as they bobbed their head to a popular Christmas song playing over the speakers. She threw her head back and laughed when Richard winked at her, and she danced with him some more.

"We should all attend the carol at the church together tonight," Richard suggested. "I am sure it'll be fun."

"I think so too," Lucy agreed.

The bell above the door rang as the door slid open and they stopped dancing when Justin came into the bakery.

"Bad time?" he asked.

"No, no, come in please," Lucy ushered him in. "How are you?"

Justin slipped his hands into his pocket and rocked back on his heels. "Compliments of the season, Lucy, and I am doing great. How are you? I should have come by sooner, but I have been swamped with work at the hotel and trying to get everything in order since the funeral and the investigation."

Hannah had turned down the music, and Aunt Tricia offered him a seat.

"I'm so sorry about what happened to Zara," Lucy consoled. "It must be hard for you to lose a daughter and wife in a short period," she said.

Justin sighed. "Zara wasn't mine," he said after a minute of silence, and she saw his eyes sink into their sockets in sadness. "She was too little to know what happened back then with her mother, but when I found out she wasn't mine and confronted her mother, she kicked me out. I left Arizona because there was nothing for me there, and when I met Tabitha, she helped me build a life. I loved her, and I knew she loved me too, even though she was rude and inconsiderate. There's no way I would have abandoned my own child, ever."

"You've been through a lot, Justin," Aunt Tricia said. She disappeared into the kitchen and returned with a glass for him. "You should join us to toast to a great year ahead."

"Both women loved me, but in the wrong way," he muttered as Aunt Tricia poured him a glass of wine.

Justin toasted with them, and they drank again. Another song came on, and Lucy sang along at the top of her voice.

On the first day of Christmas, my true love sent to me: a partridge in a pear tree...

They sang the song to the end and clapped when it ended.

"Did the cops finalize the investigation?" Richard asked.

Justin nodded. "They found the substance used to kill Tabitha in Zara's apartment and confiscated it. "It's so sad that she had to go to such lengths, poisoning Tabitha the morning before the award. It took time for the poison to work its way through her system, and she used that substance so no one would suspect it was something she ate earlier in the day. The poison killed her slowly and according to the autopsy, there was no way she would have survived the amount of poison found in her system."

Lucy shuddered, as Justin gave them details of the entire case, and Richard must have noticed this because he put his arms around her to pull her into his side for a hug.

"It's all over now, thank God," Hannah whispered.

"Yes. Both women loved me in their own way, and I just wish things turned out differently between Zara and me. Maybe if she talked to me, she would have found out the truth before she did something so diabolical."

"True," Aunt Tricia agreed. "Tabitha was not a saint, but she still did not deserve what happened to her. No one should die like that… I'm just relieved justice was served in the end, and Zara will be punished for her crimes. There are a lot of charges against her, and she will be away for a long time, maybe for life."

"Me too," Justin said. "And I'm so sorry for all that happened, Lucy. I hope we can put it all behind us and work together as agreed."

"Water under the bridge," Lucy replied with a wave of her hand. "I already signed the papers Zara came with that night, and I made a list of what I will be delivering."

"Well, it's time to put it all behind us and celebrate," Aunt Tricia said and everyone agreed. They turned on the music again and Justin thanked Lucy for welcoming him, even after everything that had transpired over the last few weeks.

"To a new start," Aunt Tricia toasted, and everyone joined her.

"We will move forward with the business as planned and will be expecting your deliveries this coming week," Justin continued, after sipping his wine.

"I can't wait to get started," Lucy replied with a smile.

That night, they attended the town's carol at the church together. Lucy sat with Richard in church and as they sang along to the carols, she hoped the new year would bring more than everything she hoped for.

The End

AFTERWORD

Thank you for reading Silent Night, Unholy Bites. I really hope you enjoyed reading it as much as I had writing it!

If you have a minute, please consider leaving a review on Amazon or the retailer where you got it.

Many thanks in advance for your support!

WHICH PIE GOES WITH MURDER?

CHAPTER 1 SNEAK PEEK

CHAPTER 1 SNEAK PEEK

The town hadn't changed much since Lucy's last visit. She noticed this when she arrived at the cemetery earlier that day for her parent's funeral. It was a short ceremony, and she had made most of the plans together with her aunt while she was in Ivy Creek. When she arrived earlier that morning, she had gone straight to the cemetery.

Her aunt drove back to her house in the neighboring town as soon as the ceremony was over, and Lucy headed back home. The first thing Lucy noticed as she arrived at her parent's house was that the front lawn was still as beautifully kept as ever. Her mother had always paid special attention to it. She had loved the beautiful burst of flowers that bloomed, especially in the summer, and Lucy had grown to love that effect too.

She got out of her car and looked around the yard, unable to wrap her mind around the death of her parents. It was sudden, painful, and destabilizing. It'd been a few days, but she already missed them.

This town, Ivy Creek, was not a place for her, and she hoped she wouldn't have to stay in town for a day longer than necessary. She had moved to the city years ago, where she had carved out a life for herself, and she was thriving there. This tragedy was the only thing bringing her back to town.

As she walked towards the front door of the house, she turned around when she heard a dog bark. She saw the next-door neighbor, Maureen Jones, a woman Lucy remembered from when she was little, walk past holding her dog on a leash.

"Lucy, dear," the woman's edgy voice boomed, the corners of her lips lifted in a smile.

Lucy forced a smile onto her face and turned around to greet Maureen.

"It's a surprise to see you in town, and a tragedy what happened to your parents. They were such a lovely couple."

Lucy greeted her with a peck on both cheeks and stepped back.

"I hope you are handling everything fine?"

"Yes, I am," she replied with another smile. "Thank you, Mrs. Jones."

The woman nodded and pulled on the leash of her dog as she walked away. Lucy turned around and walked to the house. She went right to the flower pot at the corner of the front porch, took the keys from under it, and slipped it into the keyhole to open the door.

Once inside, she looked around, and a wave of nostalgia hit her. Tears instantly filled her eyes. The last time she was here, it was Christmas, three years ago. She had made it just in time for the traditional family dinner after her mother had nagged her about it for weeks.

She felt an instant wave of guilt overwhelm her for caring less about her parents these past years. *This is my home. I grew up here, but now it feels different... empty.*

I should have visited more often.

She sucked in a deep breath, headed for the stairs in the corner. Upstairs, Lucy looked around, taking in the perfect arrangements of the smaller living room. The pictures of her when she was younger hanging on the walls, and more of her dad holding her when she had won her first award in high school on the girl's sprinting team.

Lucy wiped at her eyes gently, then took a short tour around the rest of the house. Her old bedroom was still the same, her pictures hung on the wall, and her closet remained untouched. The wallpapers she had loved so much still hung on the walls.

She dropped on the bed, and gently stroked the sheets with her hands, then sniffed. "I'm so sorry mom, and dad. I should have been here more often," she muttered to herself.

In a few hours, she would be hosting guests in the bakery, and she didn't feel like she was up to it, but she dragged herself off the bed. She spent time staring at her reflection in the full-length mirror by the corner of her bed, then went into her closet to find a pair of jeans and a T-shirt that still fit. She grabbed the keys to the bakery from her parent's room and headed out.

The drive to the bakery on one of Ivy Creek's high streets was short. The outside remained the same, with its Norman Rockwell like painting. The inside was arranged in a pattern that drew the customers to the right side where the display glasses were, and a huge menu hung on the wall, listing everything they made. Minutes later, she was inside, cleaning up and gathering baking supplies from the shelves she could use to prepare snacks for her guests. She went into the storage room and came back with everything she needed in a large bowl, then went ahead to prepare a mixture for blueberry streusel muffins and cookies.

Lucy used her mother's recipes she had learned when she was younger. She used to enjoy helping her out in the bakery a lot back then, and watching her parents work together had been fun. It was why she had successfully carved out a career in food blogging for herself and trying out new recipes was a favorite for her.

Lucy sat in the kitchen and waited after putting her dough into the oven. The bakery was still intact, and for a moment, she wondered what would happen now that they were gone. They had put so much effort and dedication into running the bakery for years, and Sweet Delights had thrived because of that.

The creamy and comforting scent of vanilla she had used in her dough filled the atmosphere, alerting her that her muffins were baked into a perfectly brown color, and as she took them out, and put in the next set, a soft knock on the front door told her the first guest had arrived.

IN ABOUT AN HOUR, the bakery was filled with citizens of Ivy Creek, some of whom Lucy recognized. They were all pleasant, chatting lightly amongst themselves as they enjoyed the confectionaries she had baked. She was proud she was able to pull it off in a few hours. Cleaning the bakery hadn't been hard at all as it was hardly ever dirty, and the majority of the work had been baking the pastries.

Lucy greeted an old friend of her father's briefly with a handshake, engaged in a light conversation with him for a few minutes before moving on to anyone else she recognized. Half an hour into the meeting, the door to the bakery opened again, and Lucy's heart did a slow dive in her chest as she noticed the man who walked in through the door. He was dressed in a black shirt tucked into navy blue jeans, and she didn't miss the gun belt on his waist. Lucy knew he had always wanted to go into law enforcement and could see he did it.

She swallowed as his eyes scanned the room, then settled on her. They stared at each other for a brief moment, and the only thing Lucy could think of at that moment was that in the five years since she last saw him, he hadn't changed one bit.

Of course, he had aged a little. His once boyish looks were gone and had been replaced with stubble that covered his face. Their gaze locked for a moment before he walked towards her. Lucy sipped from the glass she held and cleared her throat when he arrived and stood in front of her, slipping his hands into his pocket.

"Lucy Hale," he said in a low voice, his pale blue eyes not leaving hers. "It took a tragedy to bring you back home."

His statement was flat, with an underlying meaning they both understood, and Lucy plastered a smile on her face and extended a hand to him. He hesitated at first, but then slowly accepted the gesture.

"Taylor Baker—it's a pleasant surprise to have you here," she replied, and he cocked a brow. His gaze roamed her face again, and Lucy knew from the look in his eyes that he had not forgotten their history.

Taylor released her hand and slipped his back into his pocket. "Mr. and Mrs. Hale were friends of my parents too, and they are here, so it's only right that I pay my respects."

Lucy nodded, and just then Taylor's mother found them and greeted Lucy with a big hug. "Hello, Mrs. Baker."

"We are so sorry for your loss, dear," Taylor's mother whispered to her and took both her hands in hers. "It's a tragedy what happened to Morris and Kareen. They were such lovely people, the accident was a true loss for every one of us."

"Thank you," Lucy replied gently with a smile again, and Taylor whispered something to his mother before she walked away.

"So, you running again as soon as this is over?" he asked casually. "We both know Ivy Creek does not suit your exquisite needs," he added.

Her mind prepared a snappy reply to his question, but she suppressed it and nodded instead.

She didn't have the strength to get into an argument with Taylor, not at a gathering hosted in honor of her parents. All she wanted was for the night to be over, so she could slip into her bed and sleep for a long time. She was exhausted, partly because she had to stand here and accept condolences from almost everyone in town.

The gathering was her aunt's idea, and she wasn't even here to attend it because she had to get back to her daughter, who just had a baby back home.

"I don't think I'll stay," Lucy replied with a small smile, ignoring the contempt she saw in his eyes.

"I didn't think you would."

Three years ago, the Christmas she had visited, she ran into Taylor at the grocery store, and his attitude had been the same. Even though she had tried to apologize to him then, too. Lucy knew she didn't need to apologize every time they ran into each other. They had shared history, and she had chosen to move on for the sake of her career. If he couldn't forgive her for that, then there was little she could do about it.

"Thanks for paying your respects, Taylor. I appreciate it. I have to go now… to talk to other guests," she said, emptying the contents of her glass as she walked away from him, aware that his gaze was pinned on her the entire time.

She stole glances at him as he moved to join his parents in the corner of the bakery. She saw him join their conversation, and as he picked up one muffin and took a bite, she waited to see the reaction on his face.

He had enjoyed her baking once, when they were together, and he complimented it far too many times. She couldn't tell if he still thought it was good enough, and before she could look away, his gaze found hers across the room again, and lingered. He looked away first, and Lucy turned and focused on the conversation with her guests.

By the end of the gathering, Lucy cleaned up the place alone and finished late. She didn't want to go back to the main house tonight. The place held a lot of memories of her happy life there and it was painful to stay there alone.

She remembered there was a small apartment above the bakery, and as she closed the doors to the main entrance and locked the back exit, she hoped it would come in handy for her for the night. Lucy went up the stairs and flipped the light switch on, and the first thing she saw was her mother's cat, Gigi, huddled in a corner.

She bent over and touched its head as it came towards her. She let her gaze travel around the small living space, and she smiled. "This is better than I remember, and it'll be perfect."

She went in to check the bedrooms; there were two of them. It was more than enough for the night, or as long as she wished to stay. She made a trip downstairs to grab her luggage in her car, parked in the backyard. After closing her doors, she retired back to the living room upstairs to comfort herself with a cup of chamomile tea, hoping it would ease the stress of what had been quite an eventful day.

Seeing the number of locals who turned up in honor of her parents surprised her, and Taylor's presence too had shocked her, but his usual cold attitude hadn't. He was never going to forgive her. She had come to terms with that, and she could handle it.

As Lucy fell asleep, she hoped that time would heal the heaviness in her heart from her loss. When she opened her eyes the next morning, it was to the sound of something clattering downstairs. Lucy jumped out of her bed, and her heartbeat skyrocketed, leaving her with a rush of adrenaline that produced a tight knot in the pit of her stomach.

Who was out there?

WHICH PIE GOES WITH MURDER?

AN IVY CREEK COZY MYSTERY

RUTH BAKER

ALSO BY RUTH BAKER

The Ivy Creek Cozy Mystery Series

Which Pie Goes with Murder? (Book 1)

Twinkle, Twinkle, Deadly Sprinkles (Book 2)

Waffles and Scuffles (Book 3)

Silent Night, Unholy Bites (Book 4)

Waffles and Scuffles (Book 5)

NEWSLETTER SIGNUP

Want **FREE** COPIES OF FUTURE **CLEANTALES** BOOKS, FIRST NOTIFICATION OF NEW RELEASES, CONTESTS AND GIVEAWAYS?

GO TO THE LINK BELOW TO SIGN UP TO THE NEWSLETTER!

https://cleantales.com/newsletter/